Stories by Contemporary Writers from Shanghai

MEMORY
AND
OBLIVION

T0192928

This book is edited and designed by the Editorial Committee of *Cultural China* series

Text by Wang Zhousheng
Translation by Tony Blishen
Cover Image by Quanjing
Interior Design by Xue Wenqing
Cover Design by Wang Wei

Editor: Wu Yuezhou
Editorial Director: Zhang Yicong

Senior Consultants: Sun Yong, Wu Ying, Yang Xinci
Managing Director and Publisher: Wang Youbu

ISBN: 978-1-60220-244-3

Address any comments about *Memory and Oblivion* to:

Better Link Press
99 Park Ave
New York, NY 10016
USA

or

Shanghai Press and Publishing Development Company
F 7 Donghu Road, Shanghai, China (200031)
Email: comments_betterlinkpress@hotmail.com

Printed in China by Shanghai Donnelley Printing Co., Ltd.

1   3   5   7   9   10   8   6   4   2

MEMORY
AND
OBLIVION

By Wang Zhousheng

Better Link Press

Foreword

This collection of books for English readers consists of short stories and novellas published by writers based in Shanghai. Apart from a few who are immigrants to Shanghai, most of them were born in the city, from the latter part of the 1940s to the 1980s. Some of them had their works published in the late 1970s and the early 1980s; some gained recognition only in the 21st century. The older among them were the focus of the "To the Mountains and Villages" campaign in their youth, and as a result, lived and worked in the villages. The difficult paths of their lives had given them unique experiences and perspectives prior to their eventual return to Shanghai. They took up creative writing for different reasons but all share a creative urge and a love for writing. By profession, some of them are college professors, some literary editors, some directors of literary institutions, some freelance writers and some professional writers. From the individual styles of the authors and the art of their writings, readers can easily detect traces of the authors' own experiences in life, their interests, as well as their aesthetic values. Most of the works in this collection are still written in the realistic style that represents, in a painstakingly fashioned fictional world, the changes of the times in urban and rural life. Having grown up in a more open era, the younger writers have been spared the hardships experienced by their predecessors, and therefore seek greater freedom in their writing. Whatever category of writers they belong to, all of them have gained their rightful places in Chinese literary circles over the last forty years. Shanghai writers tend to favor urban narratives more than other genres of writing. Most of the works in this collection can be characterized as urban literature with Shanghai characteristics, but there are also exceptions.

Called the "Paris of the East", Shanghai was already an international metropolis in the 1920s and 30s. Being the center of China's economy, culture and literature at the time, it housed a majority of writers of importance in the history of modern Chinese literature. The list includes Lu Xun, Guo Moruo, Mao Dun and Ba Jin, who had all written and published prolifically in Shanghai. Now, with Shanghai re-emerging as a globalized metropolis, the Shanghai writers who have appeared on the literary scene in the last forty years all face new challenges and literary quests of the times. I am confident that some of the older writers will produce new masterpieces. As for the fledgling new generation of writers, we naturally expect them to go far in their long writing careers ahead of them. In due course, we will also introduce those writers who did not make it into this collection.

Wang Jiren
Series Editor

Contents

Chapter I
The Return of the Ex-husband

Had Ling Deqing known who was waiting there, she would never have opened the door. But as ill luck would have it, she did open it and then stood transfixed.

Outside the entrance to 706 Pushi Apartments stood Xiao Zichen, her husband, divorced these 20 years.

That afternoon, Ling Deqing had originally intended to go and get some medicine from the local hospital. The 77 year old retired matron's blood pressure was a little high. But the damp warmth of the March weather had tired her. She had lain down for a nap after lunch and had overslept. Suddenly, the doorbell rang loudly.

"Who is it?" she called.

Unlike the era before telephones, callers these days gave prior notice of their visits, who could this unannounced caller be?

There was no response except the insistent ringing of the bell.

Ling Deqing's doorbell was no ordinary doorbell. It was a song *Just Wait a Minute* sung by a male star. Her daughter's son, Wei Le, had installed it. Press the bell and it sang lustily: "If today could be yesterday, I would have waited a minute or a minute more and parting would not be for ever …" Her grandson had told her not to worry, if people who loved each other had a row, they should wait a minute, they wouldn't separate and could avoid the pain of parting. Ling Deqing listened in amusement and made a face, how could she believe such a shallow lyric!

Listening to the lyric she went through the living room and the kitchen to the door and asked time and again: "Who is it?"

Whoever was outside seemed not to hear and just rang the bell insistently. Each time it rang the song started again from the beginning "If today could be yesterday, I would have waited a minute or a minute more", "If today could be yesterday, I would have waited a minute or a minute more …"

How could they not reply after being asked several times? Ling Deqing hesitated by the door for a moment. She had seen the notices downstairs warning against burglars and crooks. She looked through the spy-hole but the caller was standing too close and she could only see a fuzzy shape.

Should she open the door to this silent caller or not? She stood listening indecisively.

The thick, heavy teak apartment door was probably at least 70 years old and was particularly sound-proof. Normally, there could be any amount of noise in an apartment but the corridor outside remained quiet. Ling Deqing had lived a lifetime behind this door. The light hued teak had gradually darkened over the years from its original pale honey color to its present dark brown. She had polished it times without number and one day had suddenly discovered that its color had changed, it was deeper and darker and polish as she might, it never again recovered that translucent honey color.

Oh, the passing years, she sighed, this heavy, dark brown is the passing of years!

The bell rang on incessantly: wait a minute, wait a minute more! The song became a clarion call to depression and plunged her mind into turmoil. She walked away and turned back thinking, even if it is a thief I want to look at his face and then shout stop thief; if it's not, then I really want to know who it is who understands so little of manners that they dare behave so badly.

The door creaked open.

Though she had not seen him for 20 years Ling Deqing at once recognized the man ringing the doorbell as if his life depended upon it as her former husband, Xiao Zichen.

Xiao Zichen looked at her and grinned weakly, an element of childishness in his smile, as wrinkles reached towards his temples like the opening of two flowers.

Twenty years previously, Xiao Zichen had stepped past the then honey colored door with his dark brown suitcase and had never looked back. Although they had both lived in Shanghai for the last 20 years, one had lived in this colonial era apartment on the Suzhou River and the other in post-1949 public housing, built next door to the music college on Xiangyang Road in the center of the city. They had had no contact with each other. Ling Deqing had only heard scraps of news about Xiao Zichen and his wife from her daughter.

"Why ... why have you come here?" Ling Deqing quickly recovered from her initial shock, straightened up and with a rapier-like glance, looked this former husband up and down, this man with whom she had lived together for 33 years. He was 80 now and appeared quite healthy, still with his fine face but with sparse white hair that fell loosely over his forehead. He was wearing a sleeveless light grey sweater over a crumpled white shirt; scuffed black shoes beneath dark grey western trousers, and was as untidy and unconventional as ever.

Ling Deqing glanced swiftly from side to side down the corridor, she was afraid that the neighbors would notice her former husband's arrival. Fortunately it was *siesta* time and there was no one in the corridor. As she leant out to look, Xiao Zichen stepped in saying: "I'm back, I'm back!" Ling Deqing quickly blocked the way and asked in a low voice: "Xiao Zichen, why are you here?"

Seeming not to hear her, Xiao Zichen slipped past like a child happily scampering home from school. As if he were entering uninhabited territory he went straight through the kitchen to the living room where he slumped into the coffee colored leather sofa immediately in front of the television.

Ling Deqing stood for a long time in the doorway between the kitchen and living rooms without recovering her lost wits.

Ling Deqing was half surprised, half indignant. She had been parted from her former husband for 20 years and they had not seen each other since, how could he just turn up without warning, burst in and sit on the sofa in her living room? Who did he think he was? Still the man of the house here? It was sheer wishful thinking! The Xiao Zichen of the past may have been willful and capable of childishness but he had been frightened of her and had never dared do anything that she didn't like. Do you mean to say that having been divorced for 20 years, he was no longer frightened?

Three years ago her daughter Xiao Ying had told her that Xiao Zichen's second wife, Liu Qin, had died of breast cancer. When she heard, Ling Deqing had said weakly: "That woman, what a cruel fate!" True, Liu Qin's fate had been cruel. Liu Qin's first husband had been the professor of piano at the college of music and had been "rectified" to within an inch of his life during the Cultural Revolution. He had only just survived its conclusion able to lead a peaceful life but had then suddenly developed heart disease and died. Liu Qin, the middle school music teacher who had lost her husband and her colleague, Xiao Zichen, who taught English had got together. The result? In a little over ten years she was dead. At the news of her husband's second wife's death Ling Deqing had lain on her bed thinking, how would he survive, this man totally incapable of any household task, living alone in the two room flat left him by Liu Qin? His hobby was reading, he was sociable, the moment a thought entered his head he had to find somebody he could talk to. Ling Deqing had to admit that the twice married Liu Qin was Xiao Zichen's best conversational and travelling companion, the pair's tastes were similar. Her daughter told her mother that the widowed Xiao Zichen spent each day reading, writing, and watching television but hoping that his daughter would come over. She went over every now and then with something for him to eat, but she was really too busy and when she was there, where, with all the washing and scrubbing, was the time for endless conversations with her father?

Could Xiao Zichen be thinking ... of re-marriage? The thought terrified Ling Deqing. She was totally unprepared mentally. Bearing in mind the harm that Xiao Zichen had done her, could she forgive him? Should she forgive him?

No, not at all!

Feeling the utter tedium of time, Ling Deqing sat down and waited quietly for Xiao Zichen to say something.

Xiao Zichen sat there in silence, as the sunlight moved inch by inch across the old furniture in the living room: the old mantelpiece, the German wall clock that had hung there for years, the beech wood table ...

Ling Deqing's mind was in a tangle, she stood up, went over to the glass cabinet and took out a blue and white porcelain tea bowl, poured in a few tea leaves from the old fashioned copper colored tea caddy, added some hot water from the kitchen thermos flask and put it on the tea table in front of Xiao Zichen. She had decided; first manners, then battle.

A penetrating fragrance drifted up as the curled blue-green tips rose and fell in the translucent bowl. Green Conch Spring tea? Xiao Zichen's eyes lit up, originally called "stop-you-in-your-tracks-scented" this was his favorite tea. He raised the bowl and blew, breathed in deeply and swallowed a mouthful; fragrant, really fragrant, he was in seventh heaven.

Looking at Xiao Zichen, Ling Deqing felt a sense of unfamiliarity. In the past, he had always thanked her when she handed him a bowl of tea, today he had not uttered a word of thanks.

Ling Deqing at last said: "Xiao Zichen, you came here uninvited, that's really rather impolite, I'm asking you, why are you here?"

"Er, nothing really." Xiao Zichen smiled at her inanely and carried on drinking his green tea.

"Nothing really?" Ling Deqing raised an eyebrow in astonishment.

"Came back to have a look," he added recklessly.

Ling Deqing's eyebrows shot up even further: "Have you any right to come back here?"

A flicker of fear showed in Xiao Zichen's eyes and he dropped his head.

"Xiao Zichen," she said severely. "This has not been your home for a long time, for 20 years, do you know how many days and nights there are in 20 years? You know how I endured day in day out ..." Suddenly, tears welled up and she stood and hurried to the bathroom.

Xiao Zichen put down the blue and white porcelain tea bowl, embarrassed and at a loss.

Drying her tears, Ling Deqing returned to her normal calm. She emerged from the bathroom and said coldly: "If you have something to say, then say it quickly. If not, then drink up your tea and go back to your own home."

Xiao Zichen nodded and hurriedly picked up his bowl of tea.

He slowly drank the tea, carefully tasting the flavor of every mouthful.

To Ling Deqing's astonishment he then gave her the bowl saying: "I'd like some more."

It's enough to make your head spin, give an inch and he takes a mile. Ling Deqing suppressed her astonishment, it looked as if he was intent on staying. What was to be done? She became angry: "Can't you pour it for yourself?"

The phrase "Pour it for yourself" gave Xiao Zichen the feeling that he really was home. He rose happily, strolled with familiarity into the kitchen, poured tea for himself and nonchalantly returned to the sofa.

Ling Deqing agitatedly urged him: "If you've nothing to say, drink up and go home, I've things to do!"

Xiao Zichen murmured softly in English: "To be, or not to be?"

"What do you mean?" Ling Deqing was mystified. She was aware of this phrase, so often on the lips of Xiao Zichen, the teacher of English. When she was young they were always reading Shakespeare together and had read Hamlet. But what did he mean by suddenly producing this quotation?

Existence or death? What did it mean?

Going, or staying?

Re-marriage, or not?

He was really strange. Ling Deqing stood, went into her daughter's room, closed the door and telephoned her daughter.

Ling Deqing emerged from the room after telephoning and found Xiao Zichen gazing out of the window. Outside, several white clouds floated in the clear blue sky.

"Finished your tea?" she urged him.

Xiao Zichen withdrew his gaze, looked at his bowl, saw the tea leaves on the bottom and muttered to himself: "Joy is the cause of suffering."

"What are you saying?" she asked.

Xiao Zichen raised his head and looked at Ling Deqing without replying, a fleeting expression in his eyes.

Chapter II
A Daughter's Distress

Xiao Ying took her mother's call at the office and rushed home. Strange, how could father have suddenly decided to go and see mother? Rather as if the sun was rising in the west. Her father had always been in fear of her mother and even if he had wanted to return he wouldn't have had the courage!

Truth to tell, Xiao Ying was afraid of her mother too and had never dared discuss with her in detail her relationship with her father, Xiao Zichen. Her mother had never willingly revealed her own inner thoughts. The year Xiao Ying graduated from university she had been assigned to the district library and the leadership had sent her to Beijing to study for three months. By the time she returned her parents had divorced and her father had left. During those three months away she had written often to her mother and father and to her husband, but not one of them had told her about it.

One day, after who knows how much time, her father had suddenly appeared at her office in the district library and Xiao Ying, filled with competing emotions, had burst into tears. She felt wronged, her son was nearly two and had never been hugged by his grandfather. As far as Xiao Ying was concerned, her father's role had been more that of a mother; for his part, he loved her dearly in his amiable way but her mother was like a father, cold and severe.

Xiao Ying wiped her tears and complained: "Dad, how could you and mum have done this?"

Xiao Ying then learned from her father's lips that he had not wanted to divorce but that Ling Deqing had insisted upon it. Xiao Zichen had got on well with Liu Qin, the music teacher at his school and had it been said that she had become his confidante he would not have denied it. Nevertheless, apart from exchanging anxieties there had been nothing between them. Xiao Zichen told his daughter: "Yingying, I never did anything wrong but your mother wouldn't believe it. She said that for a widowed woman to discuss her distress with a male colleague and visit his home—where in heaven could there be any purity in such a thing?" Finally, there had come a day when Ling Deqing had said to him: "I've thought it through, I give in to her, we'll separate!" Xiao Zichen had never thought of divorcing but Ling Deqing's words carried weight and there was nothing that he could do. He told his daughter: "Your mother, she's like a piece of iron, so hard it's impossible to change, there was no way out!"

Xiao Ying weighed it all up. If her husband, Wei Wenzhang was to have a female confidante she would naturally be angry and she could not condemn her mother for being heartless. However, Xiao Zichen believed that there was no right and wrong where emotions were concerned but only where morality was concerned.

Xiao Ying asked: "Well, in that case, do you feel for Liu Qin?"

Xiao Zichen nodded: "I do, but I've never done anything to be ashamed of where your mother is concerned."

"Well," Xiao Ying continued, "do you still have any feeling for mother?"

"I do!" replied Xiao Zichen without a moment's hesitation.

Xiao Ying was angered: "Do you mean to say that loving two people at the same time isn't a moral problem?"

Xiao Zichen said that if there was feeling, then there was feeling, nothing could be done about it, he hadn't done anything improper, but your mother left me no emotional leeway at all and threw me out!

"Emotional leeway?" Xiao Ying said firmly. "I wouldn't give my husband, Wei Wenzhang, this kind of 'emotional leeway'."

"Oh, Yingying!" Xiao Zichen regretted the fact that his daughter didn't understand him, feelings were invisible and intangible, how could you know anybody's heart?

"I came to tell you that Liu Qin and I are already married!"

Xiao Zichen had paid no attention to his daughter's sudden change of color and had merely concerned himself with the loneliness of his life after divorce and how attentively Liu Qin had looked after him. He said that he had never thought that he would ever live with another woman in his life, that it was Ling Deqing who had given him this opportunity and that he felt that he was very fortunate.

"Very fortunate!" Xiao Ying was enraged by what her father had said. She felt wholly aggrieved on her mother's part. "Dad, you're married and that's it, why do you push the responsibility on to mother? And why come and tell me that you're fortunate? These two years, have you thought of us at all? Do you know how I feel? If you're happy then keep it to yourself, don't say this sort of thing in front of me!"

Xiao Ying tossed her head and walked out, leaving her father hanging out to dry.

It was in this way that a rare opportunity for father and daughter to communicate had been lost.

When she got home Xiao Ying told her mother that dad had re-married. So? Her mother's expression was indifferent and there was a hint of mockery at the corners of her mouth. "I knew that he would marry that woman, he's always been a willful child."

Xiao Ying cautiously asked her mother: "When dad said that he didn't want a divorce why did you insist on throwing him out?"

Her mother said coldly: "Without a divorce, how would he have known what was good for him or not? The more he couldn't get what he wanted the better it appeared. If I hadn't got rid of him, he would have hated me, but the moment he got it, he knew the difference between good and bad!"

"Are you saying that dad and Liu Qin getting together isn't fortunate?" asked Xiao Ying.

"We'll have to see," said Ling Deqing.

Xiao Ying was frightened of her mother and rarely argued with her, but this time she could bear it no longer and asked her mother: "Tell me, mother, do you really love dad or not?"

Ling Deqing paused distractedly and asked in reply: "What do you think?"

Even though her mother had not replied directly Xiao Ying knew that her mother loved her father and loved him a great deal. Mother was impatient because the iron of her father's character could never be forged into steel. But father, it seemed, also loved mother. However, Xiao Ying felt instinctively that their love was not the same. Her mother's love for her father was that of a mother for a child, whilst her father's love was that of a man for a woman and her mother had no great need of that kind of love. Thus, these two kinds of love were, as between her mother and father, out of alignment.

"Mother," said Xiao Ying, "you knew full well that father was weak and yet you insisted on pushing him out, didn't you feel that the price was too high? It's yourself that you've harmed!"

Not once in her life had her daughter ever scolded her. Ling Deqing just listened in taciturn silence.

Xiao Ying rode her bicycle fast along the bank of the Suzhou River.

The waters of the Suzhou River flowed unhurriedly for over 100 kilometers from Lake Tai but once they reached these final three bridges, they appeared rather ponderous. The water flowed under the Zhapu Road Bridge and swirled into two turbid whirlpools, sweeping, neither fast nor slow, towards the lock-gates of the Wusong Bridge and under the world famous Garden Bridge where the Suzhou River meets the broad embrace of the Huangpu River.

Xiao Ying saw the Pushi Apartments as she turned right, past the Zhapu Road Bridge. Originally known as the Pearce Apartments it was a nine story red-brown block built in the 30s of the last century that stood on the northern bank by the Zhapu Road Bridge and towered proudly over the Suzhou River like a mettlesome horse. Now, this apartment building with its aristocratic air was gloomily submerged in a forest of restaurants and multi-colored advertisement hoardings. Its name had been changed from Pearce Apartments to Pushi Apartments, indicating that with the establishment of the new China, the world was one of joy and celebration. This was where Ling Deqing had spent her whole life and where Xiao Ying had been born and had lived for all of 49 years.

The passage-ways of the Pushi Apartments were full of bicycles and electric-powered cycles and the walls were covered with dark green post-boxes, one to each family. The old fashioned lift looked like a toothless mouth, a black cavern. This same lift had not looked like this when Xiao Ying was small.

Xiao Ying agitatedly burst out of the lift fearing that her parents would be at daggers drawn. She could sense that her father's second marriage had been happy and not as wretched as her mother had predicted. But when Liu Qin had died, the sound of the *qin* and of singing had departed with her and over the last two years her father had clearly deteriorated and she was anxious about his condition.

Xiao Ying gently opened the door, there was the sound of a Suzhou ballad from the television, a woman's voice singing softly. Xiao Ying tip-toed through the kitchen, turned into the living room and stopped, before her was a scene of beauty.

Xiao Zichen and Ling Deqing were sitting opposite each other, through the western window the rays of the setting sun fell on her mother and tiny motes of dust danced in the beams of sunlight around the hazy silhouette of her father.

Xiao Ying was moist-eyed, she had never expected ever to be able to see her father and mother sitting opposite each other like this, or to see a moment as touching.

"Mother!" called Xiao Ying softly.

"Oh, Yingying's back!" said Ling Deqing, her eyes fixed on the television.

"Dad? How came you here?" asked Xiao Ying in a tone of deliberate surprise.

Overjoyed, Xiao Zichen rose and grasped his daughter's hands, looking at her from left and right: "Yingying, I've come back, I've come back to see."

"Come back to see?" said Ling Deqing indifferently. "You've looked for several hours already, I don't know what more there is to see!"

Father and daughter smiled at each other. Xiao Ying said: "Mother, father's here and you're still watching Suzhou ballads, there's going to be a Chinese opera symposium at the library and the director is inviting you to take part and hear what's said."

Xiao Zichen at once said: "Yingying, I'll go too."

Xiao was delighted, this was more like a family, a word from mother, then father and then daughter, if Wenzhang were here too, it would be a real family atmosphere.

Xiao Ying clapped her hands, good! If father wanted to listen to Suzhou ballad opera then there was hope for it yet. She had thought it was finished but there were youngsters who were downloading the songs from the net and learning them. The river flowed east for thirty years and then west for thirty, interest in ballad opera was about to take off.

Ling Deqing shook her head, these sudden crazes always came to nothing, people nowadays rushed into things, how many people were there who really understood ballad opera? Ling Deqing looked at her watch, swept her gaze over the animated expression on Xiao Zichen's face and said that it was getting late, she had to get supper. "You," she said to Xiao Zichen, "had better be getting back, I'll get Yingying to see you off!"

Xiao Zichen stood dumbfounded, looking at his daughter in enquiry. The atmosphere was suddenly colder.

"Dad, would you like to eat before you go?" Xiao Ying wanted her father to stay to supper and asked him deliberately.

Ling Deqing snapped off the television and stood: "Yingying, if we have guests to supper we need side dishes and there are none prepared, how can we entertain a guest?"

Xiao Ying unwillingly prompted father to leave but he seemed reluctant and beamed at her mother.

Right, Xiao Ying thought helplessly, since mother won't ask him to supper, I'll see father off and take the opportunity to ask him why he came.

Ling Deqing went into the kitchen, tied on a blue flowered apron and the kitchen was soon filled with the sound of running water.

Xiao Ying gently pushed her father: "Dad, shall we go?"

Go? Go where? Father was a little surprised. Was he pretending to be stupid or was he absent minded? Afraid that he might be unhappy, Xiao Ying told him that she would go with him to the exhibition of 19th century French Impressionist painting at the weekend and would pick him up. Xiao Zichen clapped his hands in delight: "Good, good, excellent, I'll be waiting for you." Xiao Zichen's scholarly Shanghainese dialect delighted his daughter.

Xiao Ying helped her father through the kitchen. Ling Deqing was deep frying, dropping the dark green vegetables in with a hiss. "Going?" she asked without turning her head. "Going! Going!" Xiao Zichen replied. The door opened and Xiao Ying's husband, Wei Wenzhang stood there, feeling for his keys.

"Dad? Dad, how did you get here?" Wei Wenzhang was considerably astonished. Xiao Zichen laughed: "How are you Wenzhang? I came back for a look!" "Why don't you stay to supper dad?" Wenzhang asked enthusiastically. Xiao Ying gave her husband a look and said loudly that it was a long way and best to go before it got late. Seeming to understand, Wei Wenzhang said to Ling Deqing that he would see off dad too, left his bag and rushed out.

The sound of their conversation disappeared at the entrance to the lift. Ling Deqing hurriedly fried some vegetables, replaced the lid, turned down the heat, went to the door and looked down.

The Zhapu Road Bridge across the Suzhou River faced the Pushi Apartments at a distance. Pedestrians and vehicles were crossing and re-crossing it in the light that still remained from the setting sun. Ling Deqing suddenly felt sad. She and Xiao Zichen had been back and forth over that bridge she didn't know how many times, either to go for a stroll down Nanjing Road or to walk along the Suzhou River. Now, the bridge was old and they were old. The river was muddy and turbid and the bridge no longer carried their footprints, the one behind the other. Ling Deqing felt an indescribable sorrow.

The scent of Xiao Zichen remained in the living room, the two mysterious phrases he had left made Ling Deqing wonder.

To be or not to be?

Joy is the cause of suffering.

Chapter III
Alzheimer's Disease

What a good thing it would be if mother and father re-married! Xiao Ying sat in her office at the library, her thoughts in turmoil.

The telephone rang, it was the outpatients' department at the Xiangyang Hospital to say that her father had been sitting immovable in the department the whole day, they were just about to close, could she come over at once?

Xiao Ying put down the phone and rushed out of the office, inwardly blaming her mother for her callousness. She had insisted on her father leaving without letting him say what was on his mind, it had obviously upset him.

Entering the outpatients' department she spotted her father sitting in a corner by himself gazing vacantly out of the window. "Dad, how are you?" Xiao Ying touched her father. Xiao Zichen suddenly turned: "Yingying, why have you only come now? You promised to come to the hospital with me last night." Xiao Ying was baffled. "Dad, how could I have spoken to you last night? You must have been dreaming."

A middle aged woman doctor in a white coat from outpatients' came over and took Xiao Ying aside and quietly said: "You'd better take your father to Neurology or Geriatrics, he came in to outpatients' this morning, blood pressure and heart are both normal, we suggest an examination for an infarction of the brain, either that or Alzheimer's disease."

What disease? Xiao Ying was struck. "Alzheimer's disease was senile dementia," the doctor patted her arm. "Don't be alarmed, it's not definite, there are a score of conditions that present as senile dementia, cerebral atrophy and cerebral arteriosclerosis for example, they all have the same symptoms ..."

The doctor left and Xiao Ying sat there woodenly, looking at her father, her pitiable father, how could you have got this disease? You're so clever, an outstanding student from the English department of St John's University, how is it possible?

Xiao Zichen sat quietly, beaming at his daughter.

Xiao Ying helped him up, straightened his clothes, took the manila folder containing his medical notes and said sadly: "Dad, we're going home."

The taxi edged forward, Xiao Ying's mind was in confusion. Xiao Zichen sat by his daughter's side, mumbling happily. He read the English advertisements by the roadside as they flashed by: "Finger lickin' good—Kentucky Fried Chicken", "We take the world's greatest pictures—Nikon ..." Xiao Zichen had a passion for words, Chinese or foreign. The moment he opened his eyes he was searching for a book to read. Without a book, newspaper or magazine in his hand he was terrified, he was even reluctant to abandon medicine leaflets. At the moment, he seemed as happy as a sand boy reading these multi-colored words, as if he were returning from a spring outing.

Xiao Ying thought carefully, the change in her father was not a matter of one or two days. Her normally equable father had recently become irritable and suspicious. He was often forgetful and suspected the hourly paid cleaner of being light-fingered. In the last six months he had burnt out two kettles. She had bought him a kettle that whistled, but the kettle had boiled and whistled loudly, her father had seemed not to hear and that kettle had burnt out too.

Once through her father's door it was a darkened chaos. Bowls and chopsticks lay in the sink, the table and sofa were covered in books, only the polished gleaming piano that Liu Qin had played bore any semblance of life. Xiao Ying was puzzled, could it be that her father just polished the piano each day?

Xiao Ying fed her father and set about cleaning the room. The sound of singing came from the bathroom, father was washing, the singing was soft at first and then louder. She listened carefully, they were the English songs that her father loved, she knew some of them as well. How could it be dementia if he could remember so many old songs without forgetting a word? Xiao Ying hoped that it was something a little wrong mentally, he was too lonely and wanted his daughter's company.

Her father was tired from sitting all day at the hospital, he finished washing, lay comfortably in bed and was soon in the land of dreams. Xiao Ying washed his clothes and tidied the room. She decided to stay the night to be with him.

Xiao Ying lay on the sofa with Liu Qin's funeral portrait on the wall opposite. This woman who had brought such misfortune to her mother was in no way good-looking. Her eyes were small and she was too thin, it was only when she smiled that she had any charm. She could not be compared with her mother whose elegant and dignified beauty gave off the cool fragrance of the wintersweet flower. But how had this unattractive woman won such an easy victory?

Xiao Ying had hated Liu Qin believing her to be a schemer who had plotted to get close to her father. She had induced her father to make her his confidante and yet felt that she was blameless. But to love some one of the opposite sex involved physical passion, how could her mother not have been angered? No wife would allow another woman near her own husband. From what her father had said Xiao Ying had gathered that Liu Qin had given him all the love that a woman could give a man and had also given him great freedom. But for her mother, her love for her husband had been that of a mother with a child, controlling and with the final say in matters large and small.

Xiao Ying gradually drifted off to sleep. In the daze of sleep she suddenly heard a sound. Looking blearily she saw her father up and dressed going into the bathroom. A moment later she heard the sound of water and of her father washing and brushing his teeth. The clock pointed to one o'clock.

Xiao Ying rubbed her eyes, clambered up and took her father back to bed, telling him that it was the middle of the night and not time to get up yet. Xiao Zichen had to lie down and mumbled: "How can it be that it's not light yet?"

Xiao Ying was sleepy, she was disinclined to talk further with her father, she was very tired and quickly fell asleep. A little later she heard a flip-flip flop-flop noise and woke for the second time, it was the sound of slippers on the floor. Father, in his pyjamas, was walking round and round the room.

Xiao Ying asked sleepily: "Dad, why are you up again?"

Xiao Zichen replied: "I'm looking for something!" The checked pyjamas flashed to and fro in front of Xiao Ying's eyes.

"Dad, what are you looking for?" Xiao Ying quickly got up and put on the light.

Xiao Zichen said: "I'm looking for the way ..."

Looking for the way? What way? Xiao suddenly understood completely.

"The way home," said Xiao Zichen earnestly.

Xiao Ying looked at her perambulating father in alarm, heavens, he really was ill! Do you mean to say that he went backwards and forwards like this every night? What am I to do?

A sleepless night. Early next morning she took her father to the hospital and registered to see a neurologist.

Director Qin had neatly combed black hair and an apricot colored shirt peeped out from beneath his white coat, all spick and span. He gently asked Xiao Zichen a series of questions: Name? Occupation? Year of birth? Date of birth? Xiao Zichen replied fluently. Xiao Ying felt a sense of comfort. Director Qin then asked: "What did you have for breakfast this morning?" Xiao Zichen looked blankly at his daughter. On the way, Xiao Ying had bought him a hot coffee, a tiramisu cake and a croissant which he had repeatedly said were good. How could he have forgotten? She reminded him and he remembered one by one. "Never mind, never mind," said Director Qin. "Let's do a little arithmetic. 73+1?" "74." "73+2?" "75." Xiao Zichen answered a little disdainfully. When they reached 73+7, Xiao Zichen suddenly stopped: "73 plus 7 … 73 plus 7 …" He repeated with a crafty look in his eyes, tossing the question back to Director Qin: "Doctor, why don't you answer?"

Director Qin smiled: "Tell me, you're very quick!"

Xiao looked smugly at his daughter standing on one side, she forced a smile.

Next, Director Qin said that there were three things that he wanted Xiao Zichen to remember, mobile phone, clock and book. Xiao Zichen nodded: "I've remembered!" Director Qin asked several other questions and then suddenly, changing direction: "What were those three things that I asked you to remember?" Xiao Zichen was startled, what three things? He frowned, he couldn't remember. "Never mind, never mind," said Director Qin. "Let's do a little subtraction, what's 100 minus 7?" "93," replied Xiao Zichen. "And 93 minus 7?" Xiao Zichen blinked, he didn't know.

Xiao Zichen was angry and said that he didn't like arithmetic and never had! Seeing a doctor was about seeing a doctor, what was the purpose of all this nonsense?

Director Qin smiled and opened a pad of test forms, blood normal, biochemical indications, CT etc., to send Xiao Zichen for a series of tests. Xiao Ying discreetly asked: "What do you think my father has?"

Director Qin wrote a line on the medical history followed by a question mark. The line read "Alzheimer's". Director Qin said: "Early indication, senile dementia …"

"Nonsense!" Director Qin had hardly finished speaking,

Xiao Zichen was upset, "I don't have dementia, you shouldn't insult people."

Director Qin was not angered and smiled sympathetically, this was how this illness was described in Chinese medical textbooks, there was nothing he could do about it, patients sometimes reacted badly. The family should take him out for walks more, to places where there were people, he should take part in activities and converse more. "Good, next!"

On the way home, Xiao Zichen looked happily out of the window reading the English advertisements as they passed as he had done before. Xiao Ying said that she would help him find a live-in housekeeper, she said: "Dad, you're ill, there must be somebody at home with you."

"Ill. What illness have I got?" Dad already seemed to have forgotten what the doctor said, Xiao Ying gave a little sigh and said:

"Dad, you've forgotten."

"I know, I know," Xiao Zichen said. "My memory's bad, I must be getting old."

Having seen her father home, Xiao Ying visited a domestic employment agency and engaged a housekeeper, Little Jiang, a woman in her thirties from Anhui. After exchanging a few sentences Xiao Ying felt that she didn't have much to say and was honest. After agreeing wages she wanted to take her to the hospital for some tests, at the least liver function and lung photography. Little Jiang stood still and said: "If you're afraid that I have a disease, then I'm afraid you may have a disease! I'm asking you, does this old man of yours have an infectious disease?"

Xiao Ying looked blankly: "No, no, my father has a geriatric illness, it's just that his memory is bad, that's all." Xiao Ying didn't say "senile dementia" for fear of scaring Little Jiang off.

Little Jiang laughed and said bad memory was not a problem, she was quite willing as long as he was not incontinent. "To tell the truth, we country people are more afraid of illness than you city dwellers, you have health insurance, we don't, if we fall ill, it's family ruin."

It was true but Xiao Ying had never thought of it before. Looking at the same event from a different angle produced a different conclusion.

Xiao Ying took Little Jiang home to her father. When Xiao Zichen saw his daughter with a stranger he stared at Little Jiang in alarm. Xiao Ying explained her father's household tasks and Little Jiang affectionately called him grandpa. She opened the refrigerator and looked inside, it was completely empty and she went down to do some shopping.

A whole morning had passed and Xiao Ying was anxious to get to work. She reminded her father: "Little Jiang is here to look after you, you must treat her as a member of the family, do you hear?" Xiao Zichen nodded.

Just as Xiao Ying was about to go her father stopped her and pointing to Little Jiang as she went downstairs said: "Yingying, is this young woman reliable?" "Don't worry, dad," Xiao Ying said. "You've always said that if you treat people well they will treat you well."

Xiao Zichen nodded: "I know, I know."

After his daughter had disappeared from sight round the corner of the stairs, Xiao Zichen closed the door. "What was it that Yingying had said? How can I have forgotten!"

Chapter IV
The Grief of the Onlooker

Her daughter had been out all night and Ling Deqing busied herself in the kitchen preparing a bowl of bamboo shoots and chicken soup, a dish of perch, garlic and beans sprouts and an aster and bean curd salad. She managed to hear the *Just Wait a Minute* doorbell with some difficulty and quickly let her daughter in. Xiao Ying sighed "mother" in an exhausted voice, went through to the bedroom and lay on the bed.

Ling Deqing hurried in to ask: "You didn't come back last night, what's happened?"

Xiao Ying had to tell her about her father's illness.

So that was it! Ling Deqing's face gradually took on a sombre expression as she listened. How could the retired hospital matron who had graduated from Shanghai's Red House Maternity Hospital not know about Alzheimer's? With this illness it was not the patients who suffered but those close to them, it was the grief of the onlooker, the sufferers themselves had no idea.

Something clutched at Ling Deqing's heart, henceforth there would be no peace for her daughter. Xiao Ying was a mid-level cadre at the library, she had been selected for promotion and was preparing for a professional examination in English. Xiao

Zichen's illness was bound to affect her job, what was to be done?

Ling Deqing's lovingly prepared meal tasted like ashes on the tongue of her son-in-law, Wei Wenzhang. His wife lay on the bed, unwilling to get up and he and his mother-in-law sat opposite each other. In his heart Wei Wenzhang favored his father-in-law. His mother-in-law, capable and intelligent as she was, was rather overpowering and he was a little frightened of her. His father-in-law, although weak and disorganized, brimmed with talent and he liked him. When he had suddenly returned after having been divorced for 20 years, Wei Wenzhang knew intuitively that something was going to happen. But for Ling Deqing to push him out without inviting him to stay to supper, could she really hate him so much? Man and wife for thirty years, there must be grounds for some feeling still.

Xiao Ying slept on into the depth of night without having eaten. Wei Wenzhang's heart ached as he looked at her lying there. He couldn't help gently kissing her. His wife had been a gift from his mother-in-law and he treasured her beyond measure. Ling Deqing had chosen the young university student in her nursing care and had decided to entrust her daughter to him. After the engagement, Wei Wenzhang had felt a tinge of regret, the daughter of the beautiful matron Ling Deqing was not equally beautiful, Xiao Ying was tender and intelligent but rather plain.

At midnight Wei Wenzhang cooked some bamboo shoot and chicken soup, added garlic and bean sprouts and a poached egg, sprinkled it with a little sesame oil and gently woke his wife. Xiao Ying had slept for several hours and her energy was restored. The moment she opened her eyes and saw the bowl of aromatic noodles her appetite returned, but after several mouthfuls she thought of her father and put down her chopsticks. Would he be up in the night washing and brushing his teeth and walking round and round? Would he get on with Little Jiang the housekeeper? Wei Wenzhang looked tenderly at his wife as she stared into the distance and said: "Your mother told me that with this sort of illness the patient doesn't suffer, it's those that are close to them that suffer, you must accommodate nature, if your father is gradually losing his memory he may not have a care in the world."

Xiao Ying said that if somebody lost their memory, leaving just a body, what was the point?

Wei Wenzhang shook his head, if there was life, then there was memory, your father will never forget the most important things.

"What is it that somebody can never forget?" Xiao Ying asked, picking up her chopsticks. "You don't know, I saw those patients in the hospital yesterday, everyone of them like a block of wood, with no expression to their faces."

Wei Wenzhang fell silent.

"It would be good if dad could come back and live here," said Xiao Ying.

"Would your mother agree? How would it be possible unless they re-married?" Wei Wenzhang had his misgivings, besides, would they get on after so many years?

At that moment the telephone rang loudly, scaring them both. A strange female voice said: "Hello, hello, Elder Sister, it's Little Jiang, your father's really hard to look after, he'd eaten and went to bed without washing. As soon as I'd washed and cleared up and gone to bed, he woke up and started walking round in circles telling me to get up, get up and go shopping for food. However much I told him, he wouldn't listen. How can I sleep, with him like this? How can I work tomorrow like this? I'm leaving, I'm off first thing tomorrow!"

Xiao Ying listened in alarm. "Little Jiang, don't leave! My father will be better after taking his medicine for a few days."

"What's he got?" said Little Jiang. "You said it was a geriatric disorder, loss of memory, I think it's mental illness, why didn't you tell me?"

Xiao Ying said hastily: "It's not mental illness but possibly dementia, there's no final diagnosis yet, I wouldn't deceive you."

Xiao Ying tried all she could to keep Little Jiang but Little Jiang was adamant. She said: "Your father suspects I've taken his medicine, why should I take his medicine? It's not ginseng! Tomorrow he'll think I've stolen something, there's just the two of us here, how could that be cleared up?"

Xiao Ying's heart sank, if Little Jiang left, then the next housekeeper would leave too, how could this be any good? Xiao Ying asked Little Jiang to put her father on the line. The instant her father heard his daughter's voice he brightened up. "Yingying, Yingying," he said repeatedly. Xiao Ying talked to him patiently and he gradually calmed down. Xiao Ying carefully told him: "Dad, it's one o'clock in the morning, it's time to sleep. You mustn't disturb other people, all right?"

Xiao Zichen said: "What, one in the morning? How didn't I know?"

Xiao Ying said: "Little Jiang knows, don't get it wrong, you won't get it wrong if you listen to Little Jiang, Yingying is telling you to go back to bed now. When it gets light, you and Little Jiang can get up and go and buy something for breakfast and do some food shopping, all right?"

"Yes, yes," said Xiao Zichen. "Good boy. It'll be all right, I'm hanging up now."

Xiao Ying could not get back to sleep.

Every day when he woke up, Xiao Zichen always felt that there were things that he had not done. He distinctly remembered the names of people that he had met in his dreams and shouted them out. But there were others that he had vaguely met whose names he could never remember at all. Nevertheless, they had enthusiastic conversations, laughing and joking, all in English. He was always longing for something, waiting for something, but what? He couldn't say. These chaotic dreamscapes made him apprehensive.

Waking from a dream, Xiao Zichen's mind was a blank. He tried to remember the events and people in the dream but could not, all that remained were a few strange fragments. Sometimes he woke with a start in the middle of the night and hastily got up, wanting to do something but by the time that he had got dressed, he didn't know what it was that he had wanted to do. All he could do was to walk round and round in a circle, looking for something.

It was not easy for Xiao Zichen to tell his daughter about these strange thoughts. He kept these feelings hidden away. He was no fool. He had once told her a little but had seen the expression of despair in her eyes. This had dismayed him, he must have said something wrong or forgotten something. All this became a sign that indicated that they believed he was ill.

Xiao Zichen was conscious of the fact that there was something wrong with his mind but he was not resigned to it.

He sensed that it was something that was slowly eating away at his memory. At the start, he would suddenly forget a word that he had just thought of or something that he was about to do. He would rack his brain to recover the circumstances of a second earlier. Sometimes he hauled the memory back and sometimes he never found it.

He was panic-stricken.

This kind of forgetfulness was like a silkworm eating away a mulberry leaf bit by bit. First it was the disappearance of a momentary memory that was forgotten as if at the flick of the wrist, leaving neither shadow nor trace. Later it was those accumulated memories that were gradually nibbled away, turning to saw-toothed shaped mulberry leaves that became smaller and smaller. But those old memories from decades ago flashed to and fro before his eyes vividly and distinctly. A distant name or event streaked through his mind in an instant, like a fish escaping a net and raising his spirits, this was not just a leaf of memory but a branch.

A few days ago, for example, he had been sitting on the balcony in the sunshine of a spring afternoon when a vision of Pearce Apartments and his former wife flashed into his mind.

He suddenly felt that he had been away a long time and couldn't wait to get back. A powerful force urged him back to 706 Pushi Apartments as they were now called, to see his former wife Ling Deqing. He had drunk "stop-you-in-your-tracks-fragrant" Biluochun tea but he could not remember what he had said or done or how he had returned home.

Memory is like a tree. To Xiao Zichen, those distant events were like the leaves that had withstood wind and rain, proud, bold and not easily blown away. Recent people and events were like tender new leaves, at the mercy of the wind and liable to fall at a touch. Those wisps of leaves that kept falling from the tree of Xiao Zichen's memory, those tender young leaves and those new people and events damaged his recollection each time they fell, this was oblivion.

When he had got up this morning he had opened the wardrobe and tidied his clothes. He remembered that there was an important conference in Beijing. The magazine *English Language World* had invited him to attend a seminar on English language teaching materials. Where was the text of his speech? He fished out a collection of teaching plans from the corner of the bookcase and spread them over the bed. He sat down to look for the speech text and remembered that he had four classes today; quickly, find the black bag that he took to school, it had a wallet in it, where had that got to? He was puzzled and turned everything upside down as he searched. Thank heavens, he found the bag at last and stuffed in the teaching material. He reached the door and stood in a daze: what should he wear for a conference in Beijing, it was colder than Shanghai. He went back to look for a sweater. Why was it that he couldn't find that grey sweater he liked?

Agitated, Xiao Zichen lifted the telephone.

Xiao Ying was having breakfast, the telephone rang and her heart jumped. Sure enough, it was her father. He stuttered that he was going to buy a safe, she was astonished, why would he want to buy a safe? To put his sweater in, Xiao Zichen said. Xiao Ying didn't know whether to laugh or cry. Why did he want to put his sweater in a safe? Xiao Zichen said that mother had knitted the sweater for him and he couldn't let the housekeeper steal it! "Mother" was the name that Xiao Zichen used for Ling Deqing.

It's happened again! Xiao Ying's heart tightened, if Little Zhu, the new housekeeper heard him talking like this, she would be beside herself with rage. Little Jiang had left and Little Zhu had only been there a few days. Xiao Ying told him not to talk like this, if Little Zhu heard she would be upset. "It's all right, Little Zhu is still asleep," Xiao Zichen said.

Xiao Ying said: "Dad, you just can't talk about people stealing things like that, I'll help you look for the sweater next time, I'm sure we'll find it."

"But I need to go to work," said Xiao Zichen, "and I have to go to Beijing for a conference, there isn't time."

"You're already retired," Xiao Ying said. "You don't need to go to work and there's no conference in Beijing, anyhow it's summer and you don't need to wear a sweater."

Xiao Zichen was dumbfounded: "Oh, I've retired already? Of course, of course, right, Yingying, I'll hang up."

One breaker crashed on the beach after another.

Xiao Ying received a call from her father at work and rushed over to find Little Zhu, the housekeeper and her father at daggers drawn. Little Zhu was standing in the living room and her father was standing at the entrance to the bedroom. There was a pile of clothes and a woven bag on the dining table, all that Little Zhu had brought with her.

As soon as they saw Xiao Ying, both threw accusations at each other. "She was making off with my things," said one. "No such thing," said the other. "May lightning strike me dead if I've taken your things! Have a look, where's the proof? My things are all on the table."

"Look, look," cried Xiao Zichen, pointing at Little Zhu, "not only is she refusing to confess, she hit me as well!"

Little Zhu stamped her foot: "The reason I didn't let you go out was because I was afraid that you'd get lost. So stopping you is hitting you, is it?"

Xiao Ying looked helplessly from one to the other, strange that father should be so eloquent when he was having a row.

Xiao Ying desperately wanted to keep Little Zhu on. Because Xiao Zichen had reversed night and day and slept badly at night, all the previous housekeepers had left one after the other. Little Zhu came from Sichuan and had gone out to work to support a younger brother at university and was well able to bear hardship. Xiao Ying paid her more than the going rate and wanted to keep her.

Xiao Ying embraced Little Zhu: "I'm sorry father has offended you, he's lost something and I've come to help him find it, how about waiting and seeing when we've found it?"

Little Zhu wiped her tears and eyed Xiao Zichen: "It's all over some sweater! He says his mother knitted it for him, where could his mother be at his age?"

Xiao Zichen was unhappy at seeing his daughter hug Little Zhu to comfort her and strode across, pulling her hands away from Little Zhu's shoulders, and holding them in his own hands: "Yingying, you've not looked, why should you help her?"

Oh dear! "Dad, of course I've come to help you, to help you find the sweater." Xiao Ying went into the bedroom and pulled open the wardrobe door, there was a thud as something fell out and landed at her feet. She stooped to look and saw a white handkerchief with several fresh eggs wrapped in it, their yoke spreading over the floor. "Dad, what have you put eggs in the wardrobe for?"

"Going away, they're for eating on the train. Oh!" Xiao Zichen looked sadly at the smashed eggs. "What a mess!"

"Dad, these are raw eggs, they have to be boiled before you can eat them." Xiao Ying was helpless. Xiao Zichen stood there dumbly, looking at the expression of despair in his daughter's eyes.

Little Zhu bent and cleared up the broken eggs on the floor and a fishy smell pervaded the room. Xiao Ying found a pull-along suitcase in the wardrobe, opened it and looked inside, it was stuffed with clothes. She took them out one by one, the grey sweater lay in splendor at the bottom of the case.

Xiao Zichen's eyes brightened and he clapped his hands shouting: "Found it, found it, found mother's sweater!"

This grey woolen sweater was the last memento of Xiao Zichen's and Ling Deqing's 30 year marriage. When she had knitted as far as the armholes, she had decided to divorce. Ling Deqing finished it off hastily and although she would rather have not, allowed Xiao Zichen to take it with him. He had treasured it, had not worn it and it had remained hidden for 20 years.

Little Zhu, clearing up the broken eggshells in silence was ignored, her dark eyes rested on father and daughter; huh, found the sweater all right, but not a word of apology! I'm not working here any longer! She angrily packed up the luggage on the table.

Seeing that Little Zhu was determined to leave, Xiao Ying took out her purse to pay her, saying at the same time: "Dad, you've offended Little Zhu, you should apologise to her!"

"How have I offended her?" Xiao Zichen was puzzled.

Xiao Ying was stressed: "Didn't you say that she had taken your sweater?"

"Oh," Xiao Zichen remembered and nodded, "yes, yes."

"Then, dad, you should come over here and say sorry to Little Zhu." Xiao Ying felt that Little Zhu was honest, hardworking and conscientious and very much wanted to keep her. But Xiao Zichen stood there, unwilling to apologize.

Xiao Ying was furious, she gave Little Zhu her money and apologised and thanked her over again, her eyes filled with tears. She would have to go to the agency again, to whom could she unburden this pent up sense of grievance? Her resentment boiled over and the patient Xiao Ying lost her temper with her father: "Dad, didn't you always teach me that one should admit one's mistakes, but you are not willing to admit yours, you taught me to work hard, but you cause trouble all the time so that I have to come rushing over here time and again. Do you know how many days I've had to take off? Do you know how much it has interfered with my job at the library? Do you know ..." She couldn't finish and tears poured down her cheeks.

Xiao Zichen was overcome, he quickly stepped across and wiped away his daughter's tears, saying in distress: "Yingying, don't cry, Yingying, don't cry. It's your dad who is at fault."

Xiao Ying wiped her tears and pushed her father towards Little Zhu: "You made Little Zhu so angry that she wants to leave, you must say sorry to her!"

Xiao Zichen blinked and quickly said: "I'm sorry Little Zhu, I've offended a good person, I'm at fault," meanwhile taking her hand, and saying in English, "sorry, sorry, very sorry!"

Little Zhu giggled: "What's sao-lei, sao-lei?"

Xiao Ying laughed as well: "Grandpa was speaking English, it means sorry."

Little Zhu was moved by the sincerity of father and daughter. She imitated Xiao Zichen's pronunciation and said: "Sao-lei, sao-lei, Grandpa, because of sao-lei, I've decided to stay, but you mustn't offend me again!"

Laughter swept the room and the atmosphere relaxed. Little Zhu's anger subsided. She felt that the Xiao father and daughter were people of principle, she sympathized with Xiao Ying's predicament but was also mindful of her wages.

Xiao Ying was pleased beyond expectation and urged her father again and again to listen to Little Zhu. Xiao Zichen nodded away like a chicken pecking at corn: "I know, I know, don't worry, Yingying."

The office was quiet in the afternoon and Xiao Ying put her mind to revising the English reading skills from the professional English exam revision material.

The telephone rang, Xiao Ying jumped, not her father again!

It was her father of course: "Yingying, I'm a bit scared."

Scared of what? Yingying wondered.

"I can smell a strange smell," said Xiao Zichen.

"What strange smell," Xiao Ying asked. "Where's Little Zhu?"

"Little Zhu has gone out and isn't back yet," said Xiao Zichen.

Xiao Ying comforted her father: "Dad, it's probably a smell that has come in through the window from outside, Little Zhu will be back soon." Xiao Ying thought; her father was ill, he was deeply suspicious and had no sense of security, even a strange smell would frighten him.

But she had just hung up when the phone rang once more. It was her father again, he asked mysteriously: "Yingying, can you smell it, is it something burning?" Startled, Xiao Ying asked: "How can I smell something over the telephone? Did you say burning? Is the gas stove on? Dad, go into the kitchen and look now, turn the gas off at once!"

"I don't seem to have ..." said Xiao Zichen hesitantly.

"Dad!" said Xiao Ying in a loud voice. "Go when you're told to! Go and turn off the gas, now!"

Throwing down the phone, Xiao Ying rushed out, putting her head round the door of the office next door to explain to her colleague, Lao Qiao, on the way. The taxi reached Xiangyang Road in half an hour. At the bottom of the stairs she smelt the metallic odor of something burning. She climbed the stairs up to the fifth floor as fast as she could and breathlessly opened the door. The flat was filled with the acrid smell of smoke and her father was standing there in a daze, gazing out of the window.

At the sound of his daughter opening the door, Xiao Zichen smiled in delight: "Yingying's back, Yingying's back!" Xiao Ying rushed into the kitchen, it was filled with fumes and black smoke was pouring from the newly bought whistling kettle as the flame of the gas stove burnt high. Xiao Ying turned off the gas and opened the door and all the windows. "Dad, when I told you to turn off the gas, what were you doing standing at the window the whole time?"

Xiao Zichen said: "I was a bit scared and thought that you would come …"

Xiao Ying found a fan and vigorously fanned the smell out of the window saying as she did so: "Dad, who told you to boil a kettle of water by yourself?"

Xiao Zichen looked vague: "I don't remember!"

Very often, Xiao Zichen's mind opened and closed and a momentary thought would spring up, but then it would open and close again and in another moment the thought would disappear. This afternoon, he had heard footsteps like those of Liu Qin at the lift, Liu Qin was back! He knew that Liu Qin liked Biluochun tea but when he shook the thermos flask, it was empty. He hurried into the kitchen to boil some water. He lit the gas and put the kettle on. But his mind opened and closed again and the sound of footsteps in the passage disappeared, Liu Qin had not come back. He was greatly disappointed and stood gazing out of the window. Xiao Zichen really did not know from moment to moment what in his mind was true and what was false. He dared not tell his daughter this for fear that he would see that expression of despair in her eyes.

Xiao Ying hurriedly cleaned the gas-stove and the extractor fan and swept the kitchen until she perspired. Xiao Zichen stood guiltily on one side like a disobedient child. Xiao Ying was annoyed with Little Zhu and asked her father where she had gone. Why had she been away so long? Xiao Zichen was confused and couldn't explain. Just at that point Little Zhu returned, humming a tune with her pony-tail swinging behind her. She stood in the door-way, shocked.

A girl-cousin of Little Zhu's had arrived in Shanghai from Sichuan to look for work and had come to see her this morning. Little Zhu had helped Xiao Zichen get lunch and had then seen her cousin off. Xiao Ying couldn't understand why seeing her cousin off should have taken so long. When, at last, Little Zhu understood the full story, she explained that she felt that she could

not ask her cousin to lunch with grandpa in case he didn't like the
idea, but her cousin came from her home village and she could not
invite her to a meal so they had something to eat in a little eating
place and what with eating and talking time had passed.

Xiao Zichen was disturbed: "How could I have been
unhappy at your cousin eating here? You didn't ask!"

Xiao Ying said: "Dad, why should a relative of Little Zhu's
have to ask to eat? You should have taken the initiative and
invited her instead of being so petty-minded."

Litle Zhu said: "I didn't ask because I thought grandpa
would be suspicious of a stranger."

Little Zhu had some reason on her side, but this time, Xiao
Ying though that she would have to dismiss her, much could be
forgiven but this could not. Little Zhu had been away too long,
there had been no water in the thermos flask and to top it all, gas
was no laughing matter. She hadn't the heart to do so and hoped
that Little Zhu would herself realize she had lost her job. But
Little Zhu, because she was so excited at seeing a relative from
home, failed to realize. Xiao Ying had had to ask her: "Little
Zhu, do you think you can go on working here?"

Little Zhu replied: "I can, but today was my fault and I'll
mend my ways."

Xiao Zichen was listening and said: "It was my fault for not
asking Little Zhu's cousin to eat with us, Little Zhu is very good
to me, please ask her not to go."

Little Zhu's eyes reddened and at the same time Xiao Ying's
heart softened, there was no guarantee that another housekeeper
would be as good as Little Zhu, and going to the agency now
always made her tense. She was fond of Little Zhu, she was
straightforward and likeable.

As she left, Xiao Ying laid down the law to her father: "Dad,
you are not to turn on the gas."

"I know, I know," he promised repeatedly.

On the way back from her father to the Puxi library she
suddenly remembered that her afternoon computer lesson had

gone up in smoke. When was it that her life had become so fragmented and chaotic?

Could it be that life would drag monotonously on like this for ever?

In the three months since her divorced father of 20 years had suddenly reappeared at home, Xiao Ying had rushed about to the point of exhaustion. She was like a millstone, pushed by her father, that ground on and on, round and round into apathy. She was totally unaware of how the reds and purples of spring had been gradually driven further and further away by heat waves, or of how the luxuriously leafed summer had brought with it the thunder and rain that flooded the city. The results of her father's CT scan had arrived, the conclusion was quite definite: Alzheimer's disease, atrophy of the cerebellum, with some old infarction of the brain.

Xiao Zichen carefully read the instructions for his medication and was angry. "I haven't got dementia and I'm not taking this medicine!" Xiao Ying also disliked the word "dementia" it would be far better to call it "memory loss condition". Xiao Ying told her father that it was "old age illness". "But," said Xiao Zichen, "if that's the case, why should I have to take medication for dementia?" Xiao Ying was at a loss, and had to seek the assistance of the doctor each time.

At the library, Director Xu, noticing that the expression in Xiao Ying's eyes was different from before said, half sympathetically but half critically: "So busy? The balance between work and family must be managed properly!" Xiao Ying worked overtime to complete her normal work. When there was a moment, she thought of her professional English exam but as soon as she opened her English text book, her eyelids were at war.

Chapter V
The Heart of Ling Deqing

Being caught out by the unforeseen in life presented Xiao Ying with difficulties. When utterly exhausted, Xiao Ying complained inwardly: why am I my parents' only child? Why did my mother insist on a divorce?

For her part, Ling Deqing quietly scrutinized her daughter's daily activities. The wretched Xiao Zichen tormented his daughter all day, most recently over that wretched sweater when the fuss had lasted for days. What did he think he was up to, keeping it for 20 years?

During that winter 20 years ago Ling Deqing had used the evenings and weekends to knit that sweater for Xiao Zichen stitch by stitch and as she knitted she became aware of the scent of another woman in the apartment. And then, one day, unwell at work, she came home early to find a woman, a plain, long faced woman, sitting in her living room, in the midst of some weeping tale to her husband. Ling Deqing's astonishment was no trifling matter. Ling Deqing interrogated her husband: "What was this woman up to?"

"She's Liu Qin, a music teacher and colleague of mine, she plays the piano rather well."

"Are you fond of her?"

"No!" Xiao Zichen denied vigorously.

"What was she doing here?"

"Her husband's died, she was depressed and came for a chat."

"That's strange," Ling Deqing raised an eyebrow. "Her husband dies and she seeks out somebody else's husband for a chat?"

Xiao Zichen was at a loss for words. What really were his feelings for Liu Qin? He could not clearly say. Things that could not be clearly said, naturally could not be clearly explained. In fact, there was a word which was well able to explain Xiao Zichen's feelings and it was "ambiguous". When Ling Deqing had pressed him for an explanation, the greatest accusation that he had leveled at himself was that of ambiguity. Who was to know that, contrary to expectation, this had aroused even greater ire on the part of Ling Deqing.

Ling Deqing had not the heart to continue knitting the sweater. Every day she pressed Xiao Zichen for clarity and every day Xiao Zichen attempted clarity. Yet, however he attempted to explain, it was futile. To say that he was not fond of Liu Qin was clearly not true; yet to say that he was fond of Liu Qin was not entirely true either. His feeling for Liu Qin was deeper than fondness. Was it love then? Xiao Zichen did not know.

As Xiao Zichen conceived it, love ought to be a higher unity of the spiritual and physical. He enjoyed being with Liu Qin, the wide-ranging conversations and the mutual exchange of thought though, had never exceeded the bounds of spiritual contact, this was the area in which Xiao Zichen believed himself most innocent. Sometimes, during his most intimate contact with his wife, the image of Liu Qin flashed through his mind and he was suddenly startled into a feeling that he had sinned. Yet, when he was face to face with Liu Qin there were no improper thoughts. He was puzzled, where were the limits of morality to be drawn? Should those flashes of thought fall under the control of morality?

The franker Xiao Zichen became, the less able was Ling

Deqing to bear it. It was this soulful frankness that wounded her heart so deeply. How could two people who loved each other bear it when the body of one was here but the soul was elsewhere.

Xiao Zichen swore that he would have no further dealings with Liu Qin and that he would do his utmost to forget her.

Ling Deqing thought: since Xiao Zichen needed to do his "utmost" before he could "forget" that woman, wasn't that too great an effort?

As the hand rose so the knife fell, Ling Deqing cut the Gordian knot and took the greatest decision of her life: I'll realize your aim for you, let's divorce!

The consequence of Xiao Zichen's resistance was that he departed obediently. He had nowhere to go, he squeezed into the school hostel for a while and then soon moved in with Liu Qin. Liu Qin was naturally over the moon with delight. Not long after, they were formally married.

Xiao Zichen may have left but his shadow was everywhere. For a long time Ling Deqing did not know what to do for the best. At mealtimes she discovered that she had laid out an extra pair of chopsticks, at night she lacked somebody beside her to talk to; if there was a passage that she did not understand when she was reading and she decided to ask: "Oh, Zichen …" but Zichen was no longer there.

As the gathering darkness crept quietly in through the window, Ling Deqing sat in silence on the sofa and past events flitted by in the evening shadows. When, three months ago, Xiao Zichen, wearing that grey sweater, had suddenly stood on her doorstep, what had it signified?

Ling Deqing was not superstitious. But the appearance out of nowhere of this unfinished sweater of 20 years ago foretold that the love-hate relationship between her and Xiao Zichen was still unfinished.

A dish of double-boiled bamboo shoots and salted pork simmered on the hob, its aroma filling the room. Her grandson, Wei Le came home from university every weekend and Ling Deqing cooked as if for an honoured guest. The Ling family set of cups, bowls and dishes was exquisitely made, delicate dishes decorated in white, blue and white bowls and side dishes decorated with gold bordered plum blossom. Ling Deqing's cooking was appetising in any case but the reds, whites, yellows and greens served in this set looked like a table of flowers in bloom.

The family sat round the dining table eating Ling Deqing's delicious food and listening amidst ceaseless laughter to Wei Le's news from the university. Xiao Ying almost forgot the anxieties of the last few days and Ling Deqing plied her grandson with food: "Lele, eat up!"

Ling Deqing went into the kitchen and came out bearing a large translucent bowl, taking off the lid to reveal a milky white almond and tapioca pudding with a clear, slightly sweet fragrance that gladdened the heart.

Xiao Ying and Wei Wenzhang stood up to collect the bowls and chopsticks. Ling Deqing said: "Wait a moment, I have something to say." Everybody looked at her curiously and quietly sat down again.

After a moment's silence, Ling Deqing said: "I've been thinking it over and have decided that Xiao Zichen should come back and live here."

Everybody was dumbfounded. Xiao Ying looked at Wei Wenzhang and he looked at her. Wei Le looked at his father and looked at his mother and then looked at his grandmother, he didn't understand, grandmother bringing back divorced grandfather to live here, what did it mean?

Seeing everybody sitting there speechless, Ling Deqing added: "The illness Xiao Zichen has can only get worse, these last few months have worn Yingying out, she's busy at the office and I think I should help her."

Wei Wenzhang wondered, is this re-marriage? Seemingly not, thought this professor of sociology, though in fact that choosing a nursing home was the direction in which an aging society was moving. However, the family and the apartment were Ling Deqing's and he had no say in family affairs.

Xiao Ying was staggered. Wasn't this what she had always hoped for? Something that she had believed was impossible would happen. Her mother's pronouncements were written in tablets of stone. Once something was decided it never changed. But would her 78 old mother be able to cope with the toil and trouble that her father would bring with him.

"Mother," Xiao Ying was filled with mixed emotions. She stood up. "Mother," her voice trembling, "thank you," she embraced her mother. Xiao Ying could not remember how many years it had been since she had last hugged her mother. Sobbing, she buried her face in her mother's soft white hair as the tears streamed down her cheeks. Ling Deqing patted her and said: "Unless you think otherwise, it's decided, when you have time, you can go and help Xiao Zichen pack up, he'll have Lele's room and we can put up a small bed for Lele in my room which he can use at the weekend."

Ling Deqing stood and went into her room alone. That evening, she didn't come out again.

Wei Le was struck dumb. The relationship between his grandmother and his grandfather had never been of much concern to him but he had never thought that he would be the first to make a sacrifice. He would have to move out of that comfortable little room that he had occupied since he was small.

"Mother, why can't grandfather sleep in grandmother's room?" asked Wei Le. "It's got a double bed, just right for two people to sleep in."

"Idiot!" Xiao Ying said. "Grandmother and grandfather are divorced, they can't sleep in the same room."

"Huh," said Wei Le disdainfully, "they're so old, what does it matter, or you could tell them to get married again."

Xiao Ying said severely: "Lele, grandmother takes marriage very seriously, she's only having grandfather back to help reduce the burden on me, so you be good and do as she says."

Wei Le was not pleased. There was no way that he was going to sleep in the same room as his grandmother. She went to bed early and got up early, she was particular while he was completely without restraint. What was to be done?

Xiao Ying was in an awkward position. Her son was an obedient boy and had never made an unnecessary fuss. Wei Le had been the only one in the family who had dared not to sing the same tune as Ling Deqing, but in this matter he couldn't be allowed to sing a different tune. Xiao Ying said: "Lele, I'm about tired to death, grandmother is so old and yet is trying to help me, don't you think that you could make a little contribution for the sake of all of us?"

"So giving up my room to grandfather is a contribution?" Wei Le grumbled. "I didn't say that I wouldn't give up my room to grandfather, I just said I didn't want to sleep in the same room as grandmother."

Xiao Ying was in great difficulty, her mother would be displeased if she found out.

Suddenly, Wei Le slapped his forehead: "Of course, mother, I can sleep here in the living room!" He pointed to the corner by the mantelpiece, his eyes aglow.

All three looked at it, there was just room for a small bed in the corner by the mantelpiece and for a computer table under the mantelpiece. The more he looked the more Wei Le was satisfied. He extended his hand in a "V" sign, fixed!

Xiao Ying was satisfied too, she warned her son: "When grandfather comes, you must be good to him, he's ill, do you understand?"

"Understood, I guarantee to be good to grandfather!" Wei Le stuck out his chest. "But how did grandfather get this illness? Will I inherit it as well?"

Wei Wenzhang patted his arm: "This is a medical problem and a sociological one as well, if you study heredity, you can make it a research specialty of it later."

Wei Le said sadly: "Grandfather is so clever, it will really be pathetic if he forgets everything, I mustn't get this illness when I'm older."

"We must put in a great deal of research," sighed Wei Wenzhang. "These last few days, while I've been saddened at grandfather's continuous loss of memory, I've also been thinking about a different kind of memory loss, loss of national historical memory."

"Loss of national memory?" Wei Le was puzzled.

"Yes, physiological loss of memory is an individual thing. Loss of historical memory affects society. It's a major problem that will influence our development. You're no longer a child, but your understanding of contemporary history is too shallow, if the country forgets, very many tragedies will be unavoidably repeated."

Wei Le asked curiously: "Dad, are you saying that the country has forgotten something?"

Wei Wenzhang nodded: "Your grandfather is ill, he suffers memory loss, that is very sad, our society is also ill, and is also suffering memory loss. We have been forced to forget many things, including today."

Wei Le blinked. He was bewildered. What was the date today? His eyes shifted to the calendar over the mantelpiece which showed a large "4", it was June, had some major event occurred on this ordinary date?

Wei Le did not know.

Chapter VI
Who Are You?

On the way home, Xiao Zichen and his daughter were all smiles.

He asked: "Yingying, are we going home?"

"Yes, dad, mother wants you home."

And again: "Will mother scold me? I'm a bit scared."

"Mother won't scold you if you behave, so you must be good." Xiao Zichen nodded: "I'll be good, I'll be really good."

"Grandpa!" The door opened and Wei Le stood in the entrance and shouted "Welcome home, grandpa!" in English and gave his grandfather a big hug.

Xiao Zichen was delighted. Somebody had hugged him and had spoken to him in English too. This made him really happy. He stroked the sprouting beard on Wei Le's face saying: "This is a handsome young man, what's his name?"

Xiao Ying was moving luggage, an expression of sadness flashed in her eyes. "Dad, it's my son Wei Le!"

"Your son?" Xiao Zichen looked from Wei Le to his daughter. "Are you married?"

"Dad, I've been married for 20 years!"

Xiao Zichen sensed his daughter's despair and realized that

he had made another mistake. He stroked Wei Le's face again and said: "I seem to have seen this lad before!"

Wei Le turned away his head in embarrassment at being stroked and smiled a secret smile. Grandpa really was amusing, fancy asking mother such a stupid question. He had been to an art exhibition with grandpa three months ago and yet grandpa didn't recognize him. ·

Xiao Zichen came in and ran his hand over the old fashioned sofa, table and mantelpiece in the living room, sighing: "Pearce Apartments are old, really old."

Xiao Ying said: "Dad, you remember Pearce Apartments, how is it that you don't remember your grandson?"

Xiao Zichen thought earnestly for a while and said: "Lele has changed, he's got a beard, Pearce Apartments haven't changed."

For a split second, Xiao Zichen had been wide awake!

Xiao Ying and her husband and son took her father into Lele's bedroom. Lele had tidied up the single bed and the desk, the wardrobe had been divided into two, one space for himself and one for his grandfather. Xiao Ying pointed at Wei Le's bed: "Dad, this is yours."

Xiao Zichen looked at the bed carefully. So small? He bent and patted the edge of the bed: "No, this isn't my bed, mine's strung with palm fiber and very wide."

Xiao Ying and Wei Wenzhang looked at each other bemusedly. Xiao Ying quietly said: "Dad, this is Wei Le's bed, he's letting you have it and sleeping in the living room."

Xiao Zichen said obstinately: "I've always slept in a big bed, my big bed, why can't I sleep in the big bed?" walking out as he spoke.

Xiao Ying restrained him: "It's mother's arrangement, dad, you must do what she says!"

Xiao Zichen thrust his daughter aside and made for the large room that Ling Deqing occupied. Xiao Ying was unable to hold him back and the three of them followed him in.

Xiao Zichen pushed open the door, Ling Deqing was sitting

on the sofa, framed against the curtains by the bright light from the window. She was quietly reading a newspaper and at the noise, raised her head and turned to look at Xiao Zichen standing in the doorway and asked coolly: "So, you've arrived?"

Xiao Zichen was dumbfounded: "Who are you?" He turned to his daughter: "What's she doing in my room?"

Xiao Zichen was confused by the excitement.

The color drained from Ling Deqing's face as she felt an instant menacing chill. Although he was ill, she had never thought that her meeting with Xiao Zichen would begin like this. Hadn't they seen each other a mere three months ago? Had his illness progressed so fast? However, Ling Deqing was Ling Deqing and she immediately smiled and said: "Seems you've drunk Meng Po's potion of forgetfulness!"

"Dad, it's mother!" said Xiao Ying after a moment of astonishment, pushing her father and thinking: if dad didn't recognize mother it was because the light was behind her and he couldn't see. She hoped that he would greet her mother, he had used to call her "Qing" and she had called him "Zichen".

When he saw the look of despair in his daughter's eyes Xiao Zichen knew that he had once more done something wrong. He stepped forward, looked intently, gave a weak smile. "Yes, yes, it's mother. How are you?" said Xiao Zichen cautiously.

"Very well …" Ling Deqing replied extending the sound of the word.

Xiao Zichen's gaze flitted over the room and finally came to rest on the 5 foot wide bed. With its royal blue and apricot bedspread it looked soft and comfortable. Xiao Zichen pointed and said: "That's my big bed, I'm sleeping here!"

"Dad!" Xiao Ying wanted to hold her father back but he stepped forward to the side of the bed.

"Yingying," said Ling Deqing, raising her voice, "have you settled Xiao Zichen in?"

"He's settled in, we're just doing the luggage," replied Xiao Ying. "But we came to see you first."

"Then ask Xiao Zichen to go back to his own room. I need to be quiet for a while." Ling Deqing's tone of voice was particularly frigid.

Despite his reluctance, Xiao Ying tugged Xiao Zichen out of her mother's bedroom. "Dad, this is mother's room, your room is over there. You mustn't just wander in, do you hear?" Xiao Zichen took a couple of steps and stopped. He was puzzled. Why was it that mother wouldn't allow him to sleep in the big bed? Xiao Ying said: "Because you and mother are divorced. If you don't do what you're told, mother will send you back to your own home."

Xiao Zichen said: "I don't want to go back, I want to live here with you."

While Xiao Zichen was wanting to sleep in his own original big bed, Wei Wenzhang and Wei Le had quickly slipped away, they hadn't want to be spectators at an embarrassing scene and had hidden at their respective desks. Wei Le was interested by his grandmother saying that grandfather had drunk Meng Po's potion, what was it? He searched on the net: Meng Po, a beauty from Jiangnan who, after death, had been ordered by Yan Wang, the king of the underworld, to prepare a potion of forgetfulness which, when administered to those who arrived in the underworld, caused them to completely forget all the loves and hates of their previous earthly lives so that they could be re-incarnated ...

Ling Deqing sat in her own room, her emotions in turmoil. Xiao Zichen's question "Who are you?" had been like a sword that had pierced her heart and drawn blood. "Why have I had him back," she asked herself. "I could just as well have got Xiao Ying to put him into an old people's home. Why have I done this? I'm old, am I really shouldering this burden just for the sake of my pitiful daughter? Or am I doing it to make up for the guilt of having forced him into a divorce?" Thinking it over, these last few days, she had been utterly unable to clarify whether it had been for Xiao Ying or Xiao Zichen.

"Who are you?" had shattered Ling Deqing's last remaining illusion. For many years she had attempted, unsuccessfully from start to finish, to understand the question which had always dogged her: had Xiao Zichen ever truly loved her? She had pressed him on this point in the past, but he had always said: "Qing, you don't understand, you don't understand feelings and I can't explain them to you."

When he finally left, she had asked him to wait a moment, had finished off the armholes of that light grey sweater and had given it to him. He had folded it carefully, put it in his suitcase and then, putting the apartment keys gently on the dining table, had turned and left. The scene seemed to be before her still. The "thud" of the door as it closed had crushed her heart.

If, at the time, as in the doorbell's lyric "Wait a minute more", she could have changed her mind and started over again. If, at the time, Xiao Zichen had suddenly turned and pleaded through the door: "Qing, Qing, I'm not going, I don't want a divorce, can we carry on our life as we used to?" She would have leaped up and opened the door …

But there were no ifs. Xiao Zichen left and never came back. Contrary to what she had thought, his life these last 20 years had been full of interest and flavor.

Each time she heard scraps of news about Xiao Zichen from her daughter she had remained outwardly calm but her inward feelings had been complicated.

There had been an occasion when Xiao Zichen had decided on the spur of the moment to go to Dongshan near Suzhou to buy tea and Liu Qin had immediately responded and gone with him. As a result, Xiao Ying and Wei Le had missed out. Ling Deqing had been displeased when she heard. Who else, apart from Liu Qin would indulge Xiao Zichen in this way? Ling Deqing had never indulged Xiao Zichen's willfulness. She believed that you could like something but that you should never overdo it, and that to do so was a demoralizing overindulgence in triviality. Hobbies and interests could be a source of anxiety as well as pleasure. Take Biluochun tea for example. Did it matter whether or not you bought it from where it was grown? Could it really be that the Biluochun tea shipped to Shanghai from Dongshan was not Biluochun tea? Xiao Zichen found this sort of questioning extremely disheartening. He believed that Biluochun tea bought in Dongshan had a soul and that drinking it improved the mind.

Every year, Liu Qin had accompanied Xiao Zichen to Suzhou to buy tea, it was if they were on a spring outing or even a honeymoon. Ling Deqing had harbored regrets which had contained some jealousy, was she really less considerate and less romantic than Liu Qin? Her daughter blamed her for pushing her father out and she had not disputed it. Xiao Zichen had blamed her for not being able to appreciate the beauties of spring scenery and she had not disputed that either. Nevertheless, she had really given all that she felt for this man.

Ling Deqing had never discussed emotion with anybody, including her daughter. Life was not something where everything could be clearly explained.

Three months ago, her astonishment at Xiao Zichen's sudden reappearance had been followed by a daydream that Xiao Zichen had wanted to rebuild the good relationship of the past but it had turned out that he was ill. Ling Deqing had now taken him back, thinking that he would be overjoyed, that he would affectionately call her "Qing" and that he would be full of gratitude. How could she have thought that he would demand to know who she was and would attempt to seize the bed in her room to sleep in? He doesn't recognize me, he doesn't even recognize me.

Was it that she had aged so much that he didn't recognize her or that his illness had developed too quickly? Ling Deqing gently patted her grey hair and looked at herself in the mahogany dressing mirror, that elegant face had lost some of its vivacity; those deep liquid eyes no longer sparkled, her hair was streaked with grey and her skin was wrinkled.

"I'm getting old too, and should make preparations. One may fall ill with any disease but not this disease of memory loss.

An unconscious loss of dignity. People gradually regressed and became infants, just an infant housed in a body. Not knowing who they are, where they have come from or where they are going, not knowing that there are those who suffer and weep for them." At this point, she forgave Xiao Zichen. How could she have taken him for the person he had once been? That former Xiao Zichen had gradually receded into the distance and the present one was just an invalid.

The greatest tragedy for man is to live in this world and yet not to be master of one's self. Ling Deqing was nearly 80 and she feared that, like Xiao Zichen, there would suddenly come a day when she would not even recognize herself, what point was there in living like that?

Since the age of 70, Ling Deqing, the retired matron, had often considered another of life's major events; how would she die and what would be the manner of her death? What kind of trouble would her death cause her family? Although Ling Deqing had no physical disabilities she had pondered the end of life countless times. Throughout her life she had never sought favors of others and she had no intention of adding to the difficulties of her family. This consideration of old age and death through illness was not related to pessimism or to fate; precisely the opposite in fact, it was Ling Deqing's optimistic approach to the management of life.

She had sat on the sofa for the whole of the afternoon without stirring, her train of thought flying far away.

The sound of bowls and dishes penetrated the door of the bedroom and Ling Deqing broke out of her brown study; time for supper, she looked in the mirror, stood and opened the wardrobe.

In the kitchen Xiao Ying was happily busy: "Supper time!" She called as she served bean sprouts with garlic on to a dish.

Busy at their computers, Wei Wenzhang and Wei Le responded but did not move. Sniffing the fragrant smell of food, Xiao Zichen rushed happily across and dashed in and out of the kitchen continually asking his daughter if he could help. "No, no," she replied, "go and sit down."

For twenty years Xiao Ying had not believed that she would sit down to eat at the same table with her mother and father. But the day had actually arrived. She had chosen the menu with her husband and had spent much time discussing it. They had thought of everybody's favorite dishes and she had asked her mother to let her do the cooking.

The fragrant smell of cooking drifted from the kitchen into the living room where the dining table was covered in dishes. Salmon steamed in broth, spare ribs with scallion, duck marinated in bean sauce, salted green soy beans, garlic bean sprouts, boiled prawns, lettuce salad, fried bean curd and a bowl of chicken soup.

Wei Wenzhang laid out the bowls and chopsticks and Wei Le rushed in salivating with greed. He picked up his chopsticks and tasted the spare ribs but was tapped on the head by Xiao Ying: "Grandmother hasn't sat down yet!" Happily chewing the spare rib, Wei Le suddenly thought of something, went back to his computer and in a flurry of tapping on the keyboard sent his mother's menu, dish by dish, over the internet to his girl-friend, Little Hedgehog.

Little Hedgehog had been on her computer all day and the sight of the menu made her mouth water, such delicious dishes. "I'm really hungry!" She sent back a smiley with it's mouth watering: "I'd like to eat as well!" Little Hedgehog's family lived in Beijing and she couldn't get home at the weekends or eat the good food prepared by her family. Wei Le was sorry but he could not just bring a girl-friend home like that, the family would make a fuss. He comforted Little Hedgehog by telling her that next week he would invite her to eat Macao firepot just outside the university gate. Little Hedgehog sent back a laughing smiley: accepted!

After Xiao Zichen had made a fuss over wanting to sleep in the big bed, Ling Deqing had not stirred from her room the whole afternoon. This had caused Xiao Ying and Wei Wenzhang some anxiety and they signed to Wei Le to go and call his grandmother. He knocked gently at the door: "Grandma, grandma! Supper! I'm really hungry!" "Coming," replied Ling Deqing in a happy voice. Standing behind Wei Le, Xiao Ying felt relieved.

Xiao Zichen had very quickly sat down and was looking at the dishes murmuring to himself: "Prawns I like most of all and duck in bean sauce too, lettuce is good, what sort of fish is this?" He was in a hurry to pick up his chopsticks but Xiao Ying pulled at him: "Dad, wait a moment, mother's not here yet, all right?" The moment he heard, Xiao Zichen obediently put his chopsticks down.

Ling Deqing opened the door and entered the living room. She was wearing a hazy light purple silk blouse and yam dyed black silk trousers and looked remote and mysterious. Yam dyed silk was also known as fragrant cloud silk, it was quite old but still neat. Everybody's eyes brightened at the sight of Ling Deqing with her clothes set off by her white skin and elegant air. Wei Wenzhang inwardly admired his mother-in-law's sense of style, she had never had much time for brands or labels but she looked classically elegant whatever she wore. Wei Le clapped his hands and exclaimed: "Grandma! You look really pretty!"

Xiao Ying smiled: "Mother, that blouse and those trousers look really good!" Ling Deqing tapped her grandson on the head: "It's nothing to make a fuss about, they're old clothes, what's so good about them?"

Xiao Zichen looked through narrowed eyes and nodded: "Yes, yes, they're old, I've seen them before, I always said they were good looking."

Ling Deqing cheeks flushed pink and she hastily sat down, looked at the dishes in smiling appreciation and picking up her chopsticks as she spoke, said in praise: "Yingying surpasses me in cooking. Eat up, everybody!" She picked up a garlic spare rib and put it in Wei Le's bowl: "Wei Le, grandma knows that you are not keen on eating at school, so eat up at home!"

"Thank you, grandma," said Wei Le. "But I've already

stowed away one spare rib!"

"Look at the child," laughed Ling Deqing. "No manners at all!"

Xiao Zichen picked up a marinated duck leg, placed it in Ling Deqing's bowl and said affectionately: "Qing, eat!"

Ling Deqing was startled, that one word "Qing" had struck her and suddenly left her defenseless. Her head spun for a moment and she then calmed down and with a weak smile: "Zichen, you must eat as well," picked up a white prawn with her chopsticks and placed it in his bowl.

"Qing" and "Zichen", this was clearly the dinner table of twenty years ago. Everybody's heart was immediately warmed. A comfortable smile appeared on each face. Xiao Ying was so happy that her heart positively leaped. Her father had actually helped her mother to a dish! How could her father be confused one moment and clear the next? Whether it the warm family atmosphere or the fragrant smell of food, his mind had cleared in a moment.

Wei Le, with his mouth full, asked: "Grandma, what was it that you just called grandpa?"

Xiao Zichen was just about to reply when Ling Deqing said: "Lele, you mustn't talk with your mouth full, it's not polite, wait until you have swallowed."

"Is that a western custom?" said Lele. "We Chinese pay no attention to it."

Interrupted by Lele, Xiao Zichen forgot to reply.

Wei Wenzhang served a small bowl of chicken soup to everybody. Ling Deqing said: "Thank you, I'll help myself."

Xiao Zichen followed and also said: "Thank you, I'll help myself."

The soup they eat, made from a free-range hen was, in the Shanghai phrase, so fresh that it almost made your eyebrows drop out.

Chapter VII
Like or Love?

It was late at night and the clamour from the streets around Pushi Apartments had gradually subsided. Meishi Street was being cleaned, the sound of brooms, barrels and water taps blended together and the gentle sound of the laughing repartee between men and women workers was amplified by the night.

Wei Le was in a chat room on the computer. He had arranged with Little Hedghog to discuss the Golden Bear award-winning film, *Tuya's Marriage*. Little Hedgehog was a student in the Foreign Languages Department whom he had come to know on the net, they had already met face to face.

They had both downloaded the film, the plot was not complicated but the story, set in Inner Mongolia, was very moving. Tuya's husband, Batar, had lost the use of both legs when digging a well and his wife had taken on the heavy burden of the family but life was insupportable. Batar had decided upon divorce in the hope that Tuya could re-marry. In the end Tuya made the painful decision to divorce but kept Batar living with her new family.

Wei Le and Little Hedgehog had argued irreconcilably on the net about Tuya's decision. Wei Le had been moved to tears by Tuya's love but Little Hedgehog had felt that Tuya had wounded Batar's dignity and had been selfish. The two of them had excitedly debated back and forth.

Wei Le felt the tickling sensation of breath on the back of his neck, he looked round and his grandfather was standing behind him his eyes fixed on the screen.

Wei Le jumped out of his skin. Grandfather had gone to bed after supper, how had he suddenly appeared? How long had he been standing there? Wei Le was vaguely uneasy, he didn't want his grandfather to know that he had a girl friend called Little Hedgehog he had met on the net.

Wei Le urged his grandfather to go back to bed but a cheerful Xiao Zichen simply pulled up a chair beside Wei Le and smiled: "Like the children's song, let's sit in a row and eat fruit."

Wei Le was not at all pleased. Grandfather had come home and not only had he given up his room for him, now he was disturbing him at night, what was to be done?

Grandfather at night and during the day was not the same. During the day his eyes were dull and his speech wooden; at night he was bright eyed and animated. Wei Le felt ill at ease with him sitting alongside watching him chat.

Little Hegehog at the other end was anxious and tapped away: "What are you doing, why aren't you talking?"

Wei Le quckly replied: "Grandfather's with me, speak to me!"

Xiao Zichen pointed at the screen and asked: "Who's that?"

Wei Le said: "A friend."

"Boy or girl?"

Wei Le could only say: "Girl."

Xiao Zixhen nodded and asked: "Do you like her?"

Grandfather was really difficult to cope with. Grandma's attempts to control him from head to foot were already enough to bear and now there was grandfather as well. Wei Le was really peeved and said: "Grandpa, why are you asking this? It's private!"

Xiao Zichen nodded and said earnestly: "I asked whether you liked her or not. I said 'like' not 'love'! Liking and loving are not the same."

Wei Le laughed, his grandfather was really amusing: "Grandpa, you don't understand, In Shanghai 'like' is 'love', it means the same, so I can't answer your question!"

Xiao Zichen shook his head: "It's not the same, like is liking and love is loving."

Wei Le asked: "What's the difference?"

Xiao Zichen looked at the ceiling and thought: "Love is larger than heaven and like, well, like is smaller!"

A look of pleasure passed across Wei Le's face, how could grandfather be ill? "Grandpa, you're great!"

The computer pinged and the screen lit up, Little Hedgehog had sent a tearful emoticon: "It's fine for you, you have a grandfather, unfortunately I don't …"

Xiao Zichen stared at the screen: "This computer was really good to play with, I'll buy one as well some time, I like to type English." Wei Le said happily: "Good! I'll ask mother tomorrow to get you one and I'll teach you how to get on to the internet." At this, Xiao Zichen stood up and made for his daughter's room where his money was kept, he wanted to buy a computer. Wei Le stopped him: "Grandpa, it's the middle of the night, mother's asleep, let's leave it until tomorrow."

Wei Le coaxed his grandfather back into the bedroom whispering into his ear: "If old people don't sleep at night their bodies can't cope, if grandma finds out she'll be angry."

"Grandma? Who was grandma?" Xiao Zichen blinked. "If grandma was a big, bad wolf, I wouldn't be afraid!"

Wei Le nearly burst out laughing: "Grandma is Ling Deqing, are you afraid of Ling Deqing?"

Xiao Zichen said meekly: "Yes, I'm afraid of Ling Deqing."

"That's good, Ling Deqing wants you to go to sleep. If you don't, I'll tell her tomorrow."

"Please don't tell her, I'll go to sleep." Xiao Zichen obediently lay down. Wei Le switched out the light, closed the door and returned to his computer in the living room.

Little Hedgehog fired off a whole series of questions: "So late and your grandfather is still awake, what were you talking about?"

Wei Le told Little Hedgehog everything about his grandfather's illness and how his grandmother had brought back her divorced husband to live at home.

Little Hedgehog was astonished: "Your grandmother is super-great, even greater than Tuya! But you must be a little nicer to grandpa!"

"Of course, I've given up my room to him and I sleep in the living room."

"I like you for doing that!"

Like? Wei Le's heart jumped a few times and he told Little Hedgehog what his grandfather had just said: "Grandpa just said that liking and loving were not the same, liking is smaller than heaven and loving is bigger."

Little Hedgehog was silent and after a while sent: "Your grandfather doesn't seem ill!"

Suddenly Wei Le felt his neck tickling, rubbed it and felt his grandfather's chin, Xiao Zichen was up again!

"Ai-ya, grandpa, why haven't you gone to sleep?" Wei Le was really unable to manage his grandfather.

Xiao Zichen pointed at the screen: "Grandpa is me, right?"

Wei Le nodded.

"You're talking about me, right?"

Wei Le nodded again.

"Well, if you're talking about me then I can look." Xiao Zichen said contentedly.

What could Wei Le do? All he could say was: "Then have a look."

"Let me do some typing," Xiao Zichen begged his grandson. "I haven't done any typing for a long time, we used to have an English typewriter at home."

"All right, go ahead and type." Wei Le gave up his chair to his grandfather.

Xiao Zichen was over-joyed and with both hands on the keyboard said: "This keyboard isn't the same as the old English typewriter keyboard, what shall I type?" He thought with his head on one side and his fingers began to move over the keyboard, unfamiliar at first but then very naturally, clickety-clack, typed out a long string of English:

> One word is too often profaned
> For me to profane it,
> …

Xiao Zichen recited as he typed, perfect in pitch and rhythm. Wei Le stood agape. Wei Le had known from his childhood that his grandfather spoke Shanghainese with a Suzhou accent and fluent English as well. However when he spoke mandarin, Wei Le was tempted to laugh. "Shanghai Mansions" became "Shanghai Rooms", and "exhibition" became "dance display". Grandfather had taught English in a middle school and English was spoken throughout in the classes he taught. This had fascinated many upper middle school students, but unfortunately, English had not been well regarded at the time and he had become a target for criticism. He was accused of worshipping all things foreign and criticised for his English being more correct than his mandarin. Were it today, schools would be fighting to have him as an English teacher.

"Grandpa," Wei Le asked, "what poem is this?"

"It's …?" The question had caused a short circuit in Xiao Zichen's brain. He frowned and thought hard but couldn't remember, he had even forgotten what the next line was.

Xiao Zichen was a little dejected. Wei Le quickly comforted him: "It doesn't matter, grandpa, I can help you by searching for it on the net." He entered the sentence his grandfather had typed into google and clicked. There it was: "Grandpa, it's called *To* and it's by Shelley."

"That's it, that's it!" It was Xiao Zichen's turn to be excited. He stood up and looked at the computer, back and front, with his head on one side, patted it: "How can this thing be faster than a dictionary?" Wei Le laughed and said that it came over the net, search sites accumulated all sorts of knowledge and information to provide to everybody.

Wei Le then downloaded the Chinese translation of the poem and sent it to Little Hedgehog:

To
by Shelley

One word is too often profaned
For me to profane it,
One feeling too falsely disdain'd
For thee to disdain it.
One hope is too like despair
For prudence to smother,
And pity from thee more dear
Than that from another.

I can give not what men call love;
But wilt thou accept not
The worship the heart lifts above
And the Heavens reject not:
The desire of the moth for the star,
Of the night for the morrow,
The devotion to something afar
From the sphere of our sorrow?

Xiao Zichen's face was almost stuck to the screen. He read the translation carefully: "Yes, yes, very well translated!"

Little Hedgehog read the poem and immediately sent an emoticon of amazement: "Your grandfather is really great, this poem is in our English language material, it's classical English, unfortunately I don't know it by heart."

Wei Le hugged his grandfather affectionately and kissed him on the forehead thinking: how could he be ill, he has an amazing memory. Wei Le said: "Grandpa, how could you remember this poem?"

Xiao Zichen said: "A long time ago I always used to recite it to mother."

Mother? Wei Le looked blank and then recalled that when his grandfather said "mother" he was referring to grandma.

Ping, ping, Little Hedgehog flashed: "I'm now a fan of your grandfather's, I really must meet him!"

Wei Le shifted his chair a little closer to his grandfather and asked mysteriously: "Grandpa, can you tell me how you came to meet grandma?"

Without a moment's hesitation Xiao Zichen said: "She and my girlfriend were in the same dormitory."

"What, your girlfriend and grandma lived in the same dormitory?" Wei Le didn't understand: "Then how did you come to take up with grandma?"

There was a creak and Ling Deqing's door opened making Wei Le and Xiao Zichen jump with fright. Wei Le swiftly put a finger to his lips "Shh!" and both of them fell silent.

"What are you up to, so late?" Ling Deqing had been worried and had come out to look. As was to be expected not only had Wei Le not gone to bed but he had kept Xiao Zichen up as well. How could this be allowed?

"Grandma," Wei Le giggled, "I was asking grandpa for some help with English, his English is very good."

"Help with English?" Ling Deqing looked at Xiao Zichen in disbelief. "How much English does he remember?"

"Grandma," said Wei Le hastily, "grandpa can still recite English poems! Look, grandma." He pointed to the screen and read expressively:

> One word is too often profaned
> For me to profane it,
> One feeling too falsely disdain'd
> For thee to disdain
> …

Ling Deqing stood, rooted to the spot, as if struck by lightning. How well known a poem and how long ago an event! How could all this have suddenly appeared here in this room?

With her heart thumping and her blood surging Ling Deqing felt feverish. Her face was hidden in the shadow of the table lamp, Wei Le detected nothing and carried on happily reciting:

> I can give not what men call love;
> But wilt thou accept not
> The worship the heart lifts above
> …

"That's enough, don't go on, just go to bed!" said Ling Deqing turning towards her bedroom and shutting the door with a bang.

Xiao Zichen and Wei Le looked at each other. "Not good" said Xiao Zichen. "Mother's angry, time to escape!" As in the blink of an eye he disappeared into the shadows of the living room.

Wei Le sat down in front of the computer again, the story of the love between his grandfather and grandmother broken off. Wei Le felt regret.

Chapter VIII
The Child that Ling Deqing
Brought Home

Ever since Ling Deqing had allowed her former husband Xiao Zichen to return home, her orderly retired life had been thrown into confusion. After a few days of excited animation Xiao Zichen had become totally immersed in a world of his own. His condition differed by night and day, nor was it the same in wet weather or fine, with or without people and even within the space of an hour he could be alert to start with and then in the blink of an eye disappear into a haze of vagueness. He slept heavily during the day but was spirited at night and disturbed the whole family so that there was no peace. Ling Deqing had played havoc with her mind merely trying to adjust Xiao Zichen's daily routine.

Sometimes Xiao Zichen was like a three year old, charmingly obedient and clinging to Ling Deqing. Ling Deqing only had to go out for a while and he would search everywhere for her, leaning out of the window to scan anxiously below. This gave Ling Deqing some very necessary gratification. Every time she reminded him to take his medicine he obeyed. Once, he had taken his pill and took out another one and gave it to Ling Deqing:

"You have one as well!" Ling Deqing hastily waved it away: "It's your medicine, I can't take it." Who was to know that once her back was turned he had swallowed that pill as well. This had angered Ling Deqing: "You've just had one, how could you forget it?" Xiao blinked, he had forgotten that he had just taken a pill.

There were times when Xiao Zichen was like an enthusiastic young student of literature, reciting English love poetry in the living room as he had used to:

> The desire of the moth for the star,
> Of the night for the morrow ...

Or:

> How many loved your moments of glad grace
> And loved your beauty with love false or true
> But one man loved the pilgrim soul in you
> And loved the sorrows of your changing face ...

Sometimes, like a singer, he hummed romantic songs in English: "Oh, Susanna, don't you cry for me ..." These western romantic classics made Ling Deqing feel deeply estranged. Ling Deqing liked classical Chinese opera, Kunqu opera, Beijing opera and Suzhou ballad music. In Chinese opera, love was expressed through tactful implication and never so directly or openly.

The poem that Xiao Zichen had typed out on the computer that night and which Wei Le had recited so expressively, Ling Deqing had heard countless times when she had been deeply in love. The words had long been lodged at the bottom of her heart, pressed down solidly by the stones of history. Suddenly, Xiao Zichen had prised these stones apart so that her past feelings flowed to and fro in the depths of her heart making her tremble.

Sometimes, Xiao Zichen seemed like a philosopher who would unexpectedly utter a sentence or two of some abstruse philosophical theory. There had been an occasion when Ling

Deqing had sorted a pile of old clothes ready to donate to charity for disaster relief. Xiao Zichen had been looking on and had suddenly said: "Love meets sorrow."

She had waited for him to explain but he had merely looked at her blankly, mumbled something and said no more.

Sometimes Xiao Zichen was like a caged animal in a zoo, especially in the darkness of the deep night, prowling round and round the living room, his eyes gleaming with a distant light.

When Ling Deqing got up in the night and heard the flip-flop noise of slippers on the wooden floor she knew that Xiao Zichen was marching from the door to the window and back from the window to the door. Ling Deqing pushed open the door and made him go back to bed, he went unwillingly but lay down nevertheless, muttering: "How can I do it, I still can't find the way ..."

Sometimes, Xiao Zichen seemed like a man without a mind, eyes wide open but seeing nothing, clearly awake but remembering nothing. His empty eyes gazed upon some far distant place, his mind a vast vagueness.

Ling Deqing silently observed this figure, the only man that she had ever loved and thought sadly that he was no longer the Xiao Zichen of the past, that person was already long gone. These days, he was like one of the patients that she had nursed or like a child that she had brought home, who relied upon her and needed her. But this child was not a sheet of blank paper, a sheet of blank paper could have the latest and most beautiful pictures drawn upon it. Xiao Zichen's mind was not a blank sheet, it was painted with all the changes of the years, it contained something called an amyloid. This protein acted abnormally and caused a progressive degeneration of the central nervous system. Like waves on a sea shore, the illness washed at the rocks on the shore turning them white. Sometimes, fragments from the rocks of memory were thrown from the waves, people and events from their common history, suddenly striking at her heart and making her shudder. Sometimes the sea sucked the sand and shells of those memories from the crevices in the rocks and dashed them on her in an intolerable pain.

Xiao Zichen and Ling Deqing were undergoing the completely opposite process. One, wrapped in illness was gradually losing his memory; the other faced by her husband of thirty years, ceaselessly recalled sweet memories. Xiao Zichen's memories, washed away day by day, were recalled drop by drop and gradually revived in Ling Deqing's heart.

On this particular evening after supper, Ling Deqing had made Xiao Zichen sit down and watch television with her. It was a way of adjusting his habits. Left to himself, Xiao Zichen would put down his rice bowl go to his room and fall asleep to wake in the middle of the night, wash and brush his teeth, read, walk about and make a din. She wanted to train him out of this bad habit.

Shanghai Television was showing *Life and Death on the Bund*. Xiao Zichen was paying no attention, he looked left and right and had it not been for Ling Deqing, would soon have retired to his room. Suddenly he froze and stared fixedly at the screen.

"Lingjia!" he shouted.

"What did you say?" Ling Deqing said distractedly.

"Lingjia!" said Xiao Zichen, pointing to the screen.

Lingjia had been Xiao Zichen's first love. The actress on the television did indeed resemble Wang Lingjia in her student days. She had been a bosom friend of Ling Deqing's at the Shanghai Women's Medical College and had shared a dormitory with her.

Ling Deqing said gently: "That's an actress, Lingjia has not been with us for a long time."

"How can that be? See, she's looking at us." Xiao Zichen became distracted.

However much Ling Deqing attempted to explain that people on television were not live and that television dramas, like films, were filmed first and then broadcast for everybody to see, Xiao Zichen refused to believe her, saying in agitation: "Listen, listen, Lingjia's talking!"

The actress who so closely resembled Lingjia disappeared from the screen in the blink of an eye and Xiao Zichen stood up, exclaiming: "How can Lingjia leave without a word?" making for the front door as he spoke.

Ling Deqing hastily stopped him: "Where are you going?"

Xiao Zichen, carried away, strode through the kitchen to the front door and tried to open it. Ling Deqing pressed the catch, they were locked in a stalemate, one wanted to open the door and the other would not give way. Xiao Zichen's stubbornness gave him strength and he kept repeating: "I'm going to ask her, I really am going to ask her, how could she go off without a word?"

Unable to persuade him otherwise, Ling Deqing raised her voice: "Xiao Zichen, Lingjia died a long time ago! Where do you think you can find her?"

Xiao Zichen stood for a moment and then calmed down.

Xiao Ying and Wei Wenzhang had been reading in their room and had rushed out when they heard the noise: "What's the matter, what's the matter?" as they saw Ling Deqing and Xiao Zichen at daggers drawn by the front door.

Ling Deqing explained to them: "Xiao Zichen thought he saw somebody he had once known well on the television and wanted to go and see her straight away."

"Yes, yes," said Xiao Zichen. "It was Lingjia!"

"Who's Lingjia?" asked Xiao Ying.

Ling Deqing did not utter a sound, Xiao Zichen looked at her and she still did not utter. The story of Lingjia belonged to the two of them, nobody else knew.

"Come along, come along, dad, you mustn't quarrel." Xiao Ying knew that when her father was obstinate, it was useless to confront him, it was better to go along with him. "Dad, there's a lovely moon tonight and it's not too hot outside. Would you like to go and look? Shall we go for a walk along the Suzhou River?"

"Good, good," Xiao Zichen smiled sideways. He hadn't been out once in the weeks since he had returned to Pushi Apartments. Ling Deqing was afraid that he would get lost and wouldn't allow him out on his own and didn't take him with her when she went out for fear that old neighbors would gossip if they saw him.

Xiao Zichen went dutifully off for a walk with his daughter and son-in-law. "Goodbye, mother!" Xiao Zichen had utterly forgotten Lingjia by the time he said goodbye to Ling Deqing.

Ling Deqing went back and sat on the sofa, the television flickered and her mind flew into the distance: "Oh, poor Lingjia ..."

Chapter IX
The Tragedy of Wang Lingjia

Wang Lingjia was Xiao Zichen's first love.

In the summer of 1947 Ling Deqing achieved her heart's desire and passed the examination for entry into the Shanghai Women's Medical College. Her excitement knew no bounds when she saw in the distance that famous red house on Fangxie Road. The western style building with its arched windows stood in elegant tranquillity. Its forerunner had been the Ximen Women and Children's Hospital founded by the American Women's Charitable Association in 1885. After reporting in she had occupied the same dormitory as Wang Lingjia, a pretty girl from Wenzhou and they had soon become close friends. Wang Lingjia had been warm hearted and open with bewitching eyes that rippled like the sea; Ling Deqing was cool and reserved with the serene expression of a pool of water the color of jade. The two attractive girl-students soon became the cynosure of all eyes.

Wang Lingjia's boyfriend was Xiao Zichen, a third year student from the English department of St John's University. Cultured and talented he spoke Suzhou dialect and fluent English. He took up all Wang Lingjia's extra-curricular time and the two were as close as glue. Ling Deqing was a little desolate and often spent her time reading alone in the dormitory.

When the new term started after the summer holiday of the first year and the students returned one by one, there was no sign of Wang Lingjia's graceful figure. Xiao Zichen expected her every day and so did Ling Deqing. Nearly every evening Xiao Zichen crossed the city from St John's University on the Suzhou River to the Women's College. Throughout that summer Xiao Zichen had exchanged innumerable deeply affectionate letters with Wang Lingjia, how could there be no word so abruptly? Hope dissipated more and more each day. Xiao Zichen became more and more dejected and Ling Deqing was filled with sympathy for him.

More than two months later Ling Deqing suddenly received a letter from the other side of the ocean, from America; astonished, she opened it and to her surprise found it was from Lingjia.

Wang Lingjia's mother and father were influential. Seeing the spreading flames of civil war and instability, they had married their pretty daughter off to a rich overseas Chinese businessman with American nationality. Her parents had almost forced Lingjia on to the steamship and she had wept all the way to America. Her remorse at her betrayal of Xiao Zichen knew no bounds and she was ashamed of lacking the strength to disobey her parents. In the old phrase, the tree had become a boat and it was too late to turn back. She dared not face Xiao Zichen and begged Ling Deqing to pass on the news for her, she did not seek forgiveness, she only sought happiness for Xiao Zichen.

Nothing matched the desolation of that late autumn evening. Ling Deqing summoned up her courage and gave the letter to Xiao Zichen.

It was like thunder and lightning and heaven and earth split. Xiao Zichen's whole body shook and his face paled: "Oh! Oh! Why? Why didn't she give me a chance to say goodbye?" He cried, waving the letter: "Why didn't she resist her mother and father? Why? Why?"

Ling Deqing tried in every way to comfort this young man

but in the end nothing worked and she could only stand there, watching him roaring like a wounded lion and punching the wall with his fist. Finally exhausted he slumped in a chair, tears streaming down his face. Ling Deqing carefully passed him a clean white handkerchief and gently said: "There's no need to be so broken-hearted, in this world, nice girls are not confined to Lingjia alone!"

Xiao Zichen didn't take Ling Deqing's handkerchief, but took her hand instead, embracing her and sobbing silently …

In the end Ling Deqing replaced Wang Lingjia and became Xiao Zichen's girlfriend and love's wounds were healed by love. Xiao Zichen was restored to health, his face lost its pallor, his flesh filled out and they enjoyed a time of honeyed sweetness at university. One after the other they graduated and then married.

One afternoon in the spring of 1966, the doorbell rang at Ling Deqing's home. Opening the door, Ling Deqing and her husband were confronted by Wang Lingjia and an unfamiliar man. The middle-aged man was Wang Lingjia's second husband, Er Xi. He had brought Lingjia to Shanghai to consult a doctor. He wanted to be in touch with Ling Deqing beforehand.

Ling Deqing and Xiao Zichen stood, dumb-struck, at the doorway, how could this be Wang Lingjia? They could not believe their eyes, the woman standing before them was clearly frightened out of her wits. What had happened to that open, warm-hearted girl?

With lifeless eyes, Wang Lingjia stood listlessly in the doorway. Her gaze flitted over Xiao Zichen's face with neither pleasure nor remorse and then, as her gaze was caught by Ling Deqing, two tears trickled silently down her cheeks.

Ling Deqing embraced Wang Lingjia and took her into the living room.

As soon as she had sat down, Wang Lingjia asked fearfully: "Are you," indicating Xiao Zichen, "and you," indicating Ling Deqing, "party members?"

Er Xi, sitting at the side, nodded vigorously at Ling Deqing, she immediately understood and said: "Yes, Lingjia, we're both party members." In fact, neither Xiao Zichen nor Ling Deqing had ever harboured any hope of joining the party, their backgrounds and personalities had determined their lack of affinity with it.

Wang Lingjia's eyes brightened when she heard that they were both party members and as if shedding a heavy burden she said excitedly: "That's eased my mind then, I'll definitely do what the party says!"

Ling Deqing's heart broke. She knew that Wang Lingjia had had a mental breakdown.

Wang Lingjia and her rich overseas Chinese businessman had divorced soon after marrying. In 1952, full of enthusiasm for the building of the new China, she had returned to China to work and had married Er Xi, an engineer in Harbin. But wave after wave of political campaigns followed her return. She confessed time after time and wrote endless self examinations. What had she to confess? She had returned with the heart of a new-born babe and all she could confess to was loyalty to the party. But the proletariat that had seized political power wanted continuous revolution and needed to seek out fresh targets for the revolution. A rumour that Wang Lingjia was a "spy suspect" was stealthily circulated in the factory and finally caused her mental breakdown. She had unsuccessfully attempted suicide several times. Her husband Er Xi had sought permission to come to Shanghai for medical treatment and after layer upon layer of permissions had been obtained, finally succeeded.

Ling Deqing exerted every effort through various connections to find a mental health expert in Shanghai to treat Wang Lingjia. The memories of love that lay in the depths of Wang Lingjia's mind had been utterly washed away by political campaigns, all that she remembered was the sound of the party, the voice of the party.

Under the tender loving care of Ling Deqing and Xiao Zichen, Wang Lingjia gradually recovered. With the right prescription the look in her eyes revived, the color returned to her cheeks and there was a hint of a smile at the corners of her mouth. The soul returned to Lingjia's body and memory to her mind. Finally, she expressed her apologies to Xiao Zichen for having left without saying goodbye all those years ago; to Ling Deqing she expressed sincere gratitude.

This was the only time that the two couples ever met. Xiao Zichen no longer felt hatred for Wang Lingjia, only pity. His attentive care and concern for her increased. Ten glorious days passed in a moment. How could Ling Deqing and her husband know that when they solemnly saw Wang Lingjia and her husband off on the train to Harbin, it was a final farewell to Lingjia?

One day two years later, Ling Deqing received a letter from Er Xi. Lingjia had died on the 4th of May, 1968, at the age of 38, of schizophrenia and diabetes.

At the bottom of Ling Deqing's box there was a bundle of letters from Lingjia's husband, Er Xi. They described the last years and months of Lingjia's life, she could not bear to read them through to the end. Whoever read them would find no relief.

In June 1966, at the very start of the Cultural Revolution, Lingjia had been suspended from work and put under investigation, to dig out her bourgeois thinking and to confess to each and every activity in America. Lingjia's mind, only just recovered, now faced another collapse. She felt deeply guilty at her inability to mould herself into a proletarian warrior. She cut her wrists, attempted electrocution, and refused food and medicine because she felt that those who had not remolded themselves had no right to live. She believed nobody, even relatives, she believed only in the party organization. She reported to the branch secretary on her thinking, even suspicious of whether or not the branch secretary was truly loyal to Chairman Mao. The party secretary was furious and accused her: "Who knows whether you are just pretending or are really ill!" Lingjia listened in alarm, feeling, as ever, that she had not properly remolded herself.

One night, Wang Lingjia told Er Xi that she could not remold herself in time and that there was no way out. Er Xi encouraged her for a long time and she eventually calmed down.

Er Xi went to bed but suddenly heard a noise in the middle of the night. He got up, put on the light and rushed out to look, a vegetable knife lay on the ground and Lingjia's throat was covered in blood. She glared at Er Xi and said: "Where've you hidden the sharp knife? However hard I try, I can't cut my throat!"

Alarmed, Er Xi held her in his arms, fortunately the kitchen vegetable knife was blunt and Lingjia was so weak from illness that it had not caused a catastrophe. Er Xi used a towel to bandaged her and took her to hospital. The factory hospital was ten minutes from home. Lingjia refused her husband's support and marched along bravely as if in no pain at all. As she marched she asked Er Xi: "Do I look like a revolutionary? Do I look a warrior? I can withstand the test of blood, if we unite I can definitely remold!"

In the darkness, Er Xi's face was covered in tears. When they reached the entrance to the hospital, Wang Lingjia collapsed unconscious ...

The letters from Er Xi to Ling Deqing poured out everything in mourning for Lingjia. Ling Deqing wept every time she read them. She tied the bundle with yellow ribbon and kept them, like a treasure, at the bottom of the box. Whenever she looked at the letters she had the feeling that Lingjia was still on earth, living in mutual reliance with her devoted husband in that cold northern factory.

There was much that was not worth remembering, the workplace disputes that she had endured for example, and individual antagonisms, these could be forgotten. There were other things that had to be remembered at all costs, like Wang Lingjia. The life and death of Wang Lingjia was not the life and death of a single individual, it was the life and death of a whole society. If it were forgotten, the disasters that had befallen Wang Lingjia would be visited upon others. This kind of memory loss was terrifying.

As she thought, Ling Deqing felt that the differences between Xiao Zichen and herself were of no account. She could be forgotten, Xiao Zichen could be forgotten as could very many other things. It was only Wang Lingjia who could not be forgotten.

Ling Deqing did not understand politics, but on the basis of the politics that she had encountered she vaguely felt that there was a type of terrifying memory loss that caused a nation to re-live the disasters of the past and which was a thousand times more dangerous than Xiao Zichen's Alzheimer's disease. She treasured Er Xi's letters so that her daughter and son-in-law and her grandson Wei Le were aware of this history. They should know that Ling Deqing had a friend called Wang Lingjia and they should know of her tragic fate; they should know of the country's past years of chaos and of the harsh life ...

The memories of Wang Lingjia had originally been the common property of Ling Deqing and Xiao Zichen, but now, even if he did remember, he immediately forgot. Only Ling Deqing could recall them. She did not know when she would be able to describe to the next generation the joy and the never-to-be-forgotten suffering lodged in the depths of her heart.

Chapter X
Old Friends from St John's University

Ever since she had seen the English poem that Xiao Zichen had typed on the computer, Little Hedgehog had pestered Wei Le to let her meet his grandfather. This had been awkward for Wei Le. He could not bring a girlfriend home just like that, grandma and mother would make a fuss. Little Hedgehog made Wei Le bring his grandfather to the park and meet her there. She wanted to practice spoken English with him. But grandma had never allowed him out of the door for fear he would get lost, permission had to be sought. In the event, permission was sought and grandma had agreed.

When Xiao Zichen heard that he was going to the Lu Xun Park he was so excited that he could not sleep, first saying: "What shall I wear?" and then asking, "what shall I take to eat?"

Ling Deqing was angry: "Any more nonsense and you won't go at all!" The night before, she chose a cream shirt and light grey trousers for him and gave him a sleeping pill before he would quieten down. As he was about to leave, Xiao Ying found a red sunhat and put it on his head. The eye-catching red of the hat meant there was no way that her father could get lost. Xiao

Zichen preened himself in the mirror in delight: "Really smart!"

At the entrance to the park, Wei Le introduced Little Hedgehog: "Look, this is the Little Hedgehog from the net."

"Grandpa!" said Little Hedgehog, very sweetly.

"Ah," acknowledged Xiao Zichen, "Little Hedgehog, why are you called Little Hedgehog?"

"It's a net name," said Little Hedgehog.

"What's a net name?" asked Xiao Zichen.

"It's a name used on the internet," said Wei Le.

"Oh, you mean a 'style name'," corrected Xiao Zichen. "My style name is 'Zhongpu'."

Wei Le laughed: "Grandpa, that's an honorific, this is an ordinary name for use on the net."

The park was filled with the sound of music for singing and dancing, *Red strawberries are blooming*, *Katushya* and *Troika* ... Xiao Zichen plunged into the crowd, eagerly looking around with Wei Le and Little Hedgehog clinging tightly to his hands. Neither Wei Le nor Little Hedgehog liked the songs the old people sang, not one belonged to them, they were not good listening.

With an air of mystery, Xiao Zichen suddenly said: "I saw her!"

"Who?" asked Wei Le.

"Liu Qin."

Wei Le was alarmed, this was grandpa's second wife, she was dead, how could he be so confused!

Wei Le hastily pulled his grandfather away from the crowd of singers. He had heard his mother say that Liu Qin had gone to the park every morning to teach the old people to sing and grandpa had always gone with her. The sight had awoken old memories and he must miss her.

Dragged away by the two children, Xiao Zichen looked back at every step: "Where's she gone? I've just seen her. You don't need to walk so fast, all right?"

Little Hedgehog saw the "Little Bamboo Teahouse" in front of them and suggested that they went for a cup of tea. She and grandpa could practice English, Xiao Zichen immediately forgot that he had seen Liu Qin.

There were three old people seated in the teahouse, one fat, one thin and one with a head of silver hair.

They were drinking tea and talking about the weather or the plants and flowers in English. Xiao Zichen gazed around, the sound of distant singing occasionally reaching his ears, he had left his heart in the crowd. The sound of a well-known song in English came from another corner of the park and he couldn't help singing:

> Should old acquaintance be forgot,
> And never brought to mind ...

The three old men looked over at them when they heard the sound of the singing. Wei Lei was rather embarrassed and pulled at his grandfather, Xiao Zichen took no notice and instead sang louder still. The three old men could not restrain themselves and sang:

> We will take a cup of kindness yet
> For times gone by ...

At the end of the song Xiao Zichen and the three old men clapped and applauded and the proprietress of the teahouse bustled out. Wei Le and Little Hedgehog were amazed and excited.

Little Hedgehog stood and said: "Old gentlemen, can you speak English as well?"

The three old men nodded: "Yes, we're all old students of St John's University."

So they were all "Old St John's" a name that alumni of St John's University gave themselves. Wei Le and Little Hedgehog quickly pushed the two tables together and the old people each gave their university number and discovered that the three of them had been two years ahead of Xiao Zichen. The four "Old St John's" vied with each other in introducing themselves and reminiscing about life at St John's; the gentle scenery on the banks of the Suzhou River, the tall red brick tower of the university, the curling eaves of the gymnasium, Schererschewsky Hall ...

The heady fumes of history, gathered in the minds of the "Old St John's", instantly pervaded the Little Bamboo Teahouse.

In this deeply nostalgic atmosphere they started singing English songs, from *John Brown's Body* and *Battle Cry of Freedom* to *Jeannie with the Light Brown Hair* ... Sometimes they forgot the words and the sound faltered but someone always remembered and the song rang out again.

Xiao Zichen volunteered exuberantly: "I love English poetry, I can recite Yeats by heart." They all clapped and asked him to recite, he immediately stood up and recited in English:

> When you are old and gray and full of sleep
> And nodding by the fire, take down this book,
> And slowly read, and dream of the soft look
> Your eyes had once, and of their shadows deep;

He suddenly stopped in embarrassment, he had forgotten the next verse. The head of silver hair stood and helped him through:

> How many loved your moments of glad grace,
> And loved your beauty with love false or true;
> But one man loved the pilgrim soul in you,
> And loved the sorrows of your changing face ...

Amidst the enthusiastic applause two rivers of tears trickled down the cheeks of the silver-headed "Old St John's".

Outside, a passer-by asked: "What's going on in there?"

"Can it be another English corner?" asked the other.

The words "English corner" struck the ears of Little Hedgehog. How good it would be if an English corner could be set up here with the "Old St John's" as teachers who could speak English with the young. There would certainly be many young people who would be interested.

Little Hedgehog's head buzzed with the words "English corner, English corner".

A crowd of onlookers gathered at the entrance of the Little Bamboo Teahouse.

Every day since he had been to the park and met the three old St John's students, Xiao Zichen looked at the calendar, waiting for the arrival of Saturday. Each Saturday on his desk calendar was marked with a large red circle. He had marked every remaining Saturday for the rest of the year, waiting through every second and minute for Saturday when Wei Le would take him to the park.

The green leaves on the trees quietly and unobtrusively changed to red. The bamboos that surrounded the Little Bamboo Teahouse remained a brilliant dark green.

Xiao Zichen's singing and recitation in English that day had unintentionally sown a seed. In a few short months the seed had sprouted and blossomed and born heavy fruit—The Little Bamboo Teahouse English Salon.

This artistic salon for the recitation and singing of English poetry and songs had been the creation of Little Hedgehog. It was a meeting place for old people and young students who understood English. The "Old St John's" increased from the original four to eight. These spirited ancients met their friends, exchanged confidences and nostalgically recalled a common past, all in English. Many were the product of missionary schools, Yanching, Zhendan, Tongji and St John's … there was too much feeling in common that they needed to express. The young students, drawn by talk, stopped to listen, to learn the difference between American and British English and to observe the elegant gentility of this group of elderly men. Fragrance floated from the cups of coffee on the table and smoke drifted upwards from the cigars they held, the young marveling at the sound of the old people singing. This truly was an extraordinary place.

The proprietress was ecstatic! By dint of this and that she erected an awning outside the entrance, installed new tables and chairs and bought a wireless microphone. Approaching her forties, the proprietress, who had previously been heavily made-up and gaudily dressed, appeared to change personality, she now dressed soberly and elegantly, spoke softly and acquired some additional layers of reserve.

Although this special "English Language Salon" owed it's existence to Xiao Zichen, he was not much seen there. He was only allowed to go on Saturday mornings escorted by Wei Le. Every time he appeared there was uproar in the teahouse: "That's him! Eighty years old, his breath control is fine and he sings well, he recites from memory too!" Nobody had discovered that Xiao Zichen was a dementia patient. Xiao Zichen, was always cultivated and elegant and always had a smile on his face. He liked the feeling of being one of a crowd, the more people there were, the clearer his mind and the more fluent his English. With a "Master Xiao" here and a "Master Xiao" there when people met him, Xiao Zichen felt as if he had returned to the classroom podium.

Chapter XI
An Immovable Mountain

Ling Deqing was not pleased. She felt that ever since she had allowed Xiao Zichen to go to the park he had become over-adventurous.

Every morning, after she had been food shopping, Ling Deqing had emptied a basket of gleaming white rice on to the kitchen table and called: "Xiao Zichen, time to sort rice!" Xiao Zichen had emerged from his room and obediently sat down in the kitchen. But since going to the park he had hung about in his room without emerging. Ling Deqing had been in to look and discovered him staring at the calendar.

"Always sorting rice!" grumbled Xiao Zichen, obliged to follow Ling Deqing out of the room.

Sorting rice was a daily task for Ling Deqing. Ever since she had brought that child, Xiao Zichen home she had had a rice sorting assistant.

Nobody had approved of Ling Deqing having to sort rice but she had done so for several years since her retirement. This had to do with her profession and her pathological fear of germs. She could not tolerate the bits of beech, sand, millet and leaves found in the rice. Her daughter and son-in-law said that it did not matter, there was no harm in these bits and pieces and that nobody else sorted their rice. Ling Deqing was unmoved and paid no attention. Wei Le made a riddle on "Ling Deqing sorts rice"; answer as a common saying. Wei Wenzhang scratched his head but Xiao Ying laughed and said: "This shop only, no other branches!" Ling Deqing laughed as well.

Ling Deqing liked to chat with Xiao Zichen while they sorted the rice and the two of them felt a little closer as they discussed the past and the present. There was always something that linked them to all the people of their past life in common, even if their outlook had been in conflict, their character different or there had been ill feeling. As they talked of longing for relatives or yearning for home, that wide gap between their hearts gradually began to close.

But now, Xiao Zichen pushed aside the rice, resentful at his inability to complete the task in a trice. Whatever Ling Deqing said to him, he just responded by mumbling.

"What are you up to?" Ling Deqing asked more than once.

"I don't like sorting rice," Xiao Zichen said honestly.

"Impurities in the rice, especially millet contain aflatoxins which, if eaten, can cause cancer," Ling Deqing explained.

Xiao Zichen said nothing and after a while burst out: "We are all rice!"

"What do you mean, we are all rice?" said Ling Deqing curiously.

Xiao Zichen was silent.

Ling Deqing thought for a moment, then asked: "Are you saying that there are impurities in rice and faults in people and that we are the same as rice, is that it?"

Xiao Zichen nodded.

"But," said Ling Deqing, "rice is rice and people are people, the faults in people can be corrected, rice cannot rid itself of impurities by itself, they can only be got rid of by sorting."

Xiao Zichen stared at the rice on the table and said vaguely: "An immovable mountain."

"Nonsense, I don't know what you're talking about!" said Ling Deqing with great displeasure. "You make less and less sense!"

After this dispiriting experience, suddenly, one morning, Xiao Zichen was not to be found.

Xiao Zichen had never once been out on his own since he returned to 706 Pushi Apartments, even when he went for a haircut, somebody from the family went with him. But this morning he had disappeared as soon as Ling Deqing's back was turned. Written on the leaf of a notebook was the phrase:

"A funny kind of freedom."

What was this? Did it mean he was fed up with waiting here? What was he actually thinking? Ling Deqing had twice looked for him up and down the Suzhou River but there had been not a sign of him. Anxious and angry, she circled the vicinity of Pushi Apartments, and then suddenly saw him, standing in a daze beneath the large camphor tree by the south entrance to the Apartments.

At the very least the camphor tree had a history that went back fifty years. It had been there when Ling Deqing and Xiao Zichen had married, it had been small then and nobody paid it much attention. As day succeeded day over time, the tree had gradually grown taller and taller before anybody had paid any attention to its existence. Particularly in the bleak surroundings of winter it stood there on its own, its luxuriant foliage as green as ever. Even in the bitter cold its green leaves reminded people that spring was not far off. As the surrounding buildings had been demolished and rebuilt and then demolished and rebuilt again over the past decades, only the camphor tree and Pushi Apartments had stood shoulder to shoulder together in a battle of resistance against fate. Twenty years previously, in a bid to expand living space, two stories had been added to the apartments and now no more could be added but the camphor tree grew taller year by year and had reached the 7th story. People were astonished by its vigour, but with the news that Pushi Apartments were to be demolished and its inhabitants re-located its future was in imminent danger.

Elderly people gathered here to exercise every morning surrounded by tear-off plastic shopping bags filled with fish, vegetables and meat. The residents flexed their hands and stretched their legs and asked after each other, it was like a greeting to the tree as well; when the blazing sun hung in the sky and the concrete curb in its shade was packed with people avoiding the blistering heat, that was the tree's return greeting and response to the people.

"Xiao Zichen!" shouted Ling Deqing as she puffed forward. "What are you doing here? You had me frightened to death!"

Xiao Zichen started, a light of panic in his eyes.

"Come on, what are you doing here?"

"I'm …" stammered Xiao Zichen.

However much Ling Deqing interrogated him, Xiao Zichen remained silent. Ling Deqing lost her temper: "You know you're ill, if you go out you must tell me so I know where you're going. What would happen if you got lost?"

Xiao Zichen argued: "I know my way round here."

Ling Deqing guessed that he had intended to go to the park, he was so self-indulgent!

When Xiao Zichen and Liu Qin had been married they used to go to the nearby Xiangyang Park every day. After Liu Qin retired all her interest was devoted to teaching a group of old people in the park to sing and Xiao Zichen had always accompanied her. The park was a meeting place for retired old people who came from the area of the Music College, all possessed of some skill and who liked singing and dancing. Perhaps her decision to allow Xiao Zichen to go to the park with Wei Le had been a mistake that had revived Xiao Zichen's memories of Liu Qin, leaving him unsettled.

Ling Deqing regretted her decision.

Another week arrived, Xiao Zichen anticipated and looked forward all week to the day at last when Wei Le came home. Wei Le told his grandfather that the topic for the English Salon this time would be Russian poetry and folksong and that Little Hedgehog had already downloaded and copied the English language material ready for distribution.

Xiao Zichen, beaming with delight, ran to and fro between his room and the living room, asking Wei Le: "What's the time? Shouldn't we be going now?"

But, Ling Deqing suddenly announced: "Xiao Zichen is not going to the park now and Xiao Zichen is not going to the park again!"

This was a blow and Wei Le was upset: "Grandma, why? We've always been back on time."

Ling Deqing sat on the sofa noisily turning the pages of a newspaper and said: "If he goes to the park a lot grandpa gets over-adventurous and can't settle at home. A few days ago he crept out by himself and it took me a long time to find him, it's very unsafe."

"No, no, I won't get lost," Xiao Zichen said hastily.

Wei Le hugged his grandmother and begged: "Grandma, let grandpa go, we're going to an English class, English is very important for me."

Ling Deqing looked at Wei Le over her spectacles: "It would be the same if you studied at home, wouldn't it?"

Wei Le pouted: "Grandma, it wouldn't be the same at all, it's the English Salon. There are a lot of people practicing listening to and speaking English. Besides, grandpa is very important there, everybody likes him, he's a kind of star, people wait for him every day."

"Wait for him?" Ling Deqing raised her head and looked at Wei Le. "Waiting for you more like, that Little Hedgehog, is she your girlfriend? She's always waiting for you, isn't that the case?"

Little Hedgehog? Wei Le looked at his grandmother, Xiao Zichen adopted an air of innocence. Wei Le knew that his grandfather reported everything to his grandmother despite his repeated promises not to say anything about Little Hedgehog but how could grandpa withstand grandma's relentless questioning?

Wei Le was a little embarrassed: "Grandma, she's not a girlfriend, she's a fellow student!"

Ling Deqing laughed: "With so many girl students, why

couldn't you go to the English Salon with somebody else?"

There was nothing that Wei Le could say but he still wanted to stand up for his grandfather: "Grandma, whatever you think, you ought to give grandpa a little freedom and not keep him in the whole time."

Ling Deqing was displeased: "How have I not given grandpa freedom? He's free at home, letting him go out freely wouldn't do, the traffic outside is so noisy that if he gets it wrong he'll get lost. Oh, by the way, Xiao Zichen, explain to me what you wrote in that note book, 'A funny kind of freedom', what does a funny sort of freedom mean?"

Xiao Zichen was puzzled, he had utterly forgotten what he had written in the notebook.

Grandma's word was law. Wei Le had to go by himself.

Xiao Zichen stood at the window anxiously watching Wei Le come out of the main entrance of Pushi Apartments, cross the road and disappear into the crowd on the street.

Depressed at being unable to go to the English Salon, Xiao Zichen went to his room and fell asleep.

Ling Deqing went in and saw that written in the open note book on his desk was the line:

"I've put on the light to let her know that I am awake."

What was all this? Ling Deqing was mystified. Was this riddle-like phrase from a poem or was it something that he had thought up himself, she could not work it out.

Ling Deqing wouldn't let Xiao Zichen sleep in the morning and woke him, making him get up and do some housework, polishing the table and sweeping the floor. Xiao Zichen rose very unwillingly. He took a cloth, squeezed out dishwashing liquid and polished the surface of the ornamented table backwards and forwards to a satiny shine.

Ling Deqing frowned: "There's nothing marvelous about washing up liquid, why have you squeezed out so much?"

Xiao Zichen said nothing, picked up the cloth and took it into the kitchen to rinse. He turned on the tap and rinsed it back and forth producing a lot of bubbles, this didn't rinse out the cloth but filled the sink with bubbles.

Xiao Zichen turned his attention to the bubbles in the sink and, full of interest, cupped his hands to catch the water from the tap. The water flowed noisily through his fingers down into the drain.

Xiao Zichen suddenly heard music amidst all the noise of the water. His face relaxed and his heart beat faster. He stopped rinsing and let the water play on the cloth in his hand, the sound of the water flowing through his hands and the sound of the water in the basin were different ... an emotional and unrestrained music. The wonderful sound of the water, this touching symphony, enchanted him. Xiao Zichen's anxious soul was opened.

Moved by this little pleasure, Xiao Zichen changed the position of his hands under the tap, the palm, the top of his hand, fingers spread, the tips of the fingers opposite each other, water flowing and splashing through the fretwork of interlaced fingers ...

Xiao Zichen pick up a stainless steel pan and let the water play on its top and then bottom, peng, peng, ping, ping ... head cocked, he listened carefully, yes, that was the sound of the *qin,* the sound that he knew so well, he was over-joyed.

"Are you playing with water?" Seeing that he had spent so long in the kitchen washing the duster Ling Deqing had gone in to look. "So old and still playing with water?" she scolded. "Isn't a waste of water to have the tap on so full?"

Xiao Zichen came to his senses, he hadn't heard Ling Deqing, he only heard the sound of the water and saw the water splashing on his hands.

"What are you up to?" Ling Deqing turned off the tap, giving Xiao Zichen a fright so that he woke up.

"Look at you, you've been wringing out that cloth for hours, the dishwashing liquid on the table has dried out!"

"Qing, listen," Xiao Zichen turned the tap on again and stretched out his hands to receive the water. "Listen to the *qin*!"

"What did you say?" Ling Deqing had been happy to hear him

say "Qing", for days he had been calling her "mother", impossible to correct and then suddenly, at some click of a switch in the brain he had called her "Qing", that intimate name from the past.

A happy smile appeared on Xiao Zichen's face: "Qing, the sound of the *qin,* it's yours!"

"*Qin* sound? Mine?" Ling Deqing asked doubtfully. "What's mine?"

She knew that Xiao Zichen was prone to auditory and visual hallucination. She had intended to tell him that it was the sound of the water and that he was hallucinating but having been affectionately called "Qing" twice she said nothing and just passed it off by nodding: "So you feel that the sound of water is pleasant do you? We ought to save water rather than playing with it like children."

Ling Deqing turned off the tap again as she spoke.

The sound of the *qin* disappeared and Xiao Zichen was disappointed. He had clearly seen the strange expression on Ling Deqing's face. It had rather resembled the expression of despair on his daughter's face and each time he had always done something wrong.

"Much better not to have said anything, I'll keep the sound of the *qin* in my heart, better that only I hear it!" Xiao Zichen regretted. "This was my discovery and my secret, I heard the sound of the *qin,* it was Liu Qin playing, I heard it as clearly as anything."

Xiao Zichen had lived back at home for several months and Ling Deqing felt more and more a stranger. After the initial excitement, Xiao Zichen had always presented her with a timid smile. Ling Deqing knew that he was afraid of her and she hated it. Why was he afraid, what was there to be afraid of? Wasn't everything she did for his sake? When she had been a nurse there had not been a single patient who had not spoken well of her. She treated Xiao Zichen much better than she had treated her patients. She had been extremely polite and tactful with her patients but with Xiao Zichen she could be more blunt. But when

Xiao Zichen looked at Ling Deqing, there was always fear in his eyes. She so hoped that Xiao Zichen would argue, or row with her as he had in the past, or display bad temper, at least there would be some intimacy in that.

Xiao Zichen had only to call her "Qing" occasionally and she would be happy, as if transported back to the passionate love of the past. There had even been an occasion when Xiao Zichen had pecked her on the cheek and her heart had leaped. Could it be that Ling Deqing longed for a return to the past?

But gradually, Xiao Zichen started to become depressed, the expression in his eyes was evasive, and whatever you asked him, he was vague and could not answer sensibly. Ling Deqing believed that his condition was progressively worsening but when she saw the happy expression on his face when he was with Wei Le, the robust singing of English songs, the fluent English conversation and the soft Suzhou dialect, her heart turned to ashes. Oh, Xiao Zichen, I brought you back out of the goodness of my heart, why do you always present the tearful face of a put upon daughter-in-law?

"Qing, the sound of the *qin,* it's yours!" Ling Deqing mulled over what Xiao Zichen had just said. He had taken the running water to be the sound of the *qin* and said that it was hers, but she couldn't play the *qin* and had never been able to, and Xiao Zichen knew it, so why say "The sound of the *qin,* it's yours!"

Could it be that Xiao Zichen had said "Qin" instead of "Qing"? Ling Deqing's heart fell.

The idea pierced her heart like an arrow of ice and rendered her immobile with heartache. How could she have not thought of this before? The pronunciation of her "Qing" and Liu Qin's "Qin" were very similar, there was only the difference in the final consonant and in the Shanghai dialect they sounded exactly the same.

However, when Xiao Zichen had called her "Qing" how much of "Qin" had there been in it?

"How can I have been so stupid! All along, it had been that woman Liu Qin that Xiao Zichen had never for a moment forgotten."

Chapter XII
Xiao Zichen Goes Missing

L ing Deqing phoned her daughter at the office straight away: "Yingying, your father's missing! His bed's made, the desk's tidy and there's something strange written in his notebook, listen:

> A river run dry.
> A funny kind of freedom.
> Silence is not golden.
> Hypnos lives in a mysterious cave on the northern coast of the Black Sea.
> There is just the dim light of morning and the shadows of evening.
> At the bottom of the cave the river Lethe flows.
> At the mouth of the cave, poppies grow and soporific herbs …"

"Don't go on, mum, we'll go and look for him." Xiao Ying cut off her mother. Ling Deqing had said that she had been out to look for him several times but no trace was to be found.

Xiao Ying was worried, she had reassured her mother by saying that he might have gone out because he was bored, to meet friends or to chat and would soon be back. He had a note of the address in his trouser pocket and, in any case, he knew the area and could not get lost.

Xiao Ying thought for a moment as she put down the phone, neither her mother nor father had mobile phones. Her mother didn't want a phone and her father was incapable of learning how to use one. But these days it was a nuisance to be without one. She had never asked for a holiday since her father had returned, today she had no alternative but to ask the director for a day off to go and look for her father.

Her father was most likely to have gone to the park, he really enjoyed the English Salon and her mother should not have stopped him from going.

Xiao Ying texted her husband arranging to meet at the park and to look together.

The loudspeaker in the park announced continuously: "Attention please! Would Mr. Xiao Zichen please come to the park office as soon as he hears this, his family is looking for him ..."

Xiao Ying searched every nook and cranny of the park as well as visiting the Little Bamboo Teahouse. The friendly proprietress, hearing that they were looking for Teacher Xiao who sang English songs, kept on saying: "How could he be ill, you really couldn't see it at all! He certainly hadn't been today, last Saturday there had been people asking after the old upper class Shanghai gentleman who sang English songs, why hadn't he come? Your father was always smiling, like an elderly child, everybody liked him."

Xiao Ying was worried to death.

Wei Wenzhang finished teaching and hurried out, he had had a premonition that this would happen, sooner or later, ever since Xiao Zichen had returned. He had suggested that he should go into an old people's home but the family had not agreed.

Wei Wenzhang had no right of speech in 706 Pushi Apartments. And why? It was to do with the apartment. When he and Xiao Ying had first married and there had been a housing crisis, they had smoothly moved into his mother-in-law's Pushi

Apartments much to the envy of their homeless married friends. It was only after they moved in that Wei Wenzhang discovered that all good things come at a price. It was Ling Deqing's apartment, Ling Deqing's home and Ling Deqing was its formidable mistress, and he, always a guest in the home, had the feeling that he was sheltering beneath somebody else's hedge. As soon as he was through the door home from work, he was constrained. Living at close quarters with his mother-in-law was inhibiting.

Could it be that Wei Wenzhang would spend a lifetime trapped like this on account of the apartment? He buried this feeling in the very depths of his mind; to express it would frighten both his wife and mother-in-law: who ever said that because the apartment wasn't yours you had no say? Xiao Ying and Ling Deqing had never contemplated the idea! Ling Deqing had marked him out, he had been an appendicitis patient on her ward, he was much to her liking and she had treated him like a son. His wife loved him and supported him in everything, how could he not know when he was well off and yet at the same time suffer this indefinable feeling? To be in the midst of good fortune and not to know it!

Wei Wenzhang had been brought up on a post-1949 municipal housing estate and in love with Xiao Ying, he had marveled at this elegant western-style apartment where even the bathroom and kitchen had been bigger than the rooms in his own home. Nevertheless, moving into the apartment after they were married he felt depressed. He felt like a well-treated poor relation in the household of the rich, ever obliged to feel grateful.

How much better it could be if he had his own home!

He did not know how many times this idea had occurred to him. It had been difficult to foresee the future commodification of property when he had discussed with his wife the possibility buying a flat with a loan. Xiao Ying had been baffled: "Buy a flat? Do you want to move out? How would mother cope if she were left here on her own?"

Wei Wenzhang did not dare raise the subject again for fear of being suspected of wishing to abandon the elderly. When, many years later, everybody seemed to be buying property though many were not buying it to live in but as a capital investment, Wei Wenzhang discovered that he had lost out by failing to buy. He had raised the subject again but property prices had soared and they lacked the means.

Who knows how many honest people like Wei Wenzhang and Xiao Ying there must have been in Shanghai who had dreamed of buying a home and who in the end had been unable to buy as much as a square foot.

Thinking about property, Wei Wenzhang arrived at the park entrance. Xiao Ying called from a distance. Dad had not been found, she had phoned every one of his friends, nothing, she was worried stiff!

"Calm down, calm down," Wei Wenzhang mopped away the perspiration for his wife. "Let's think about it carefully."

Wei Wenzhang asked his wife: "Do you feel dad has been happy since he came home?"

Xiao Ying started: "There's no reason for him not to be, his life's all taken care of, we've been that good to him!"

"Nevertheless," Wei Wenzhang continued, "perhaps he feels that he's not as independent as he used to be," using his own feelings at having lived with his mother-in-law for several decades to guess at his father-in-law's misery.

The remark reminded Xiao Ying: "Well, yes, mother did tell me that dad had written a lot of nonsense, something about 'an insurmountable mountain', 'a funny kind of freedom', 'silence is not golden', Mother said it had been copied from poems."

Copied or not, this was interesting. Wei Wenzhang was appreciative: "Think about it, a funny kind of freedom, he felt hedged in."

Xiao Ying nodded: "Yes, mother is too strict with him, especially not letting him go to the English Salon, he was very unhappy."

If he had no freedom here, then where would he be free? Wei Wenzhang reflected, it would be in his own home, he had gone home to Liu Qin!

Chapter XIII
Memory Is a Meeting Place

Xiao Zichen, where could he have got to? Ling Deqing gazed around on the Suzhou River. She was 78 and had searched hither and thither all over the place, she was red-faced and bathed in sweat.

Could he have gone back to Liu Qin's place on Xiangyang Road? As soon as the thought occurred to her, even though she may not have believed it, her anger knew no bounds. "You heartless fellow, going off without a word, are you trying to vex me to death? If you don't want to live at home, just say so, I won't keep you, cannot keep you! But you must tell me so." Ling Deqing stood at the roadside trying to get herself together, thinking: "I must get him back and ask him face to face, in what way have I mistreated you?"

Ling Deqing had never been to Liu Qin's flat but knew in which lane off Xiangyang Road it was and the number. She had extremely complicated feelings about Liu Qin, the woman who had stolen her husband away. She had always believed that Xiao Zichen and Liu Qin could never be happy together, that Xiao Zichen would regret having left her and that he would return and beg her forgiveness.

However, he didn't and never had! The pair of them, Xiao Zichen and Liu Qin had led a full life.

He had always been a pleasure seeking child, and all he wanted was a playmate! The proud Ling Deqing's feelings for Xiao Zichen were a tangled web of the unbreakable threads of the sorrows of parting which she could not define even to herself.

Ling Deqing hailed a cab and rushed straight to Xiangyang Road.

It was already late. The passageways of the building were silent and the sound-operated lights switched off after a few seconds. She climbed slowly to the fifth floor, no burglar proof door had been fitted to Liu Qin's flat No. 501, it was just an apricot colored wooden door set in a dilapidated door frame.

Ling Deqing tapped on the door, it was slightly ajar, why was it not locked? What was up?

"Xiao Zichen!" she called gently as she pushed open the door and walked straight in.

In the darkness, Ling Deqing bumped into a chair and then a table. Feeling her way unevenly along the wall she found a switch. A click and the light came on, a silver energy saving bulb with a cold light. It was a small sitting room of 7 or 8 square metres, an eye-catching shiny black piano stood in front of the window.

The door to the bedroom stood open, Ling Deqing peeped in, a figure lay on the bed, sure enough it was Xiao Zichen. He lay curled across the bed with his back to her, snoring gently.

Ling Deqing's heart was in her mouth but settled at long last. What was Xiao Zichen doing back here? Fetching something or just for a sleep? Could it be that he would never leave here again?

Ling Deqing switched on the dim ceiling light and silently observed the bedroom scene.

A black and white wedding photograph of Xiao Zichen and Liu Qin on silk hung at the head of the bed. On the opposite wall hung Liu Qin's funeral photograph in a black frame. When she had come across Liu Qin at home that time, her appearance had been engraved on her heart, small and delicate, rather plain looking but with some charm. In the wedding photograph she smiled broadly with closed lips and dancing eyes. Xiao Zichen, in the western suit she knew so well, was the picture of scholarly elegance.

That year, the moment when that photograph of Xiao Zichen and Liu Qin had been taken was the moment when Ling Deqing's heart had been torn asunder. When she had heard the news 20 years ago it had been as if her heart had been devoured by ants. What was it that had enabled such an ordinary woman to conquer Xiao Zichen's heart? This man huddled on the bed that she had both loved and hated and with whom she had been entwined for a lifetime, why had she given him shelter? What was she actually hoping for?

The room, shut up for a long time, gave off the smell of mould and the gloomy light dimly shone through the strange atmosphere. A black framed photograph of a cultivated looking man in glasses stood on the bedside table. Ling Deqing guessed that it was Liu Qin's first husband, professor of piano at the school of music. Alongside the photograph was a thick book, *The Collected Poems of W. B. Yeats*, with a slip of paper tucked into it. Opening the book, Ling Deqing saw that the slip had that phrase "An immovable mountain" written on it.

What nonsense was this? The writing was still fresh, could it have just been written?

What did "an immovable mountain" mean? Could it mean his illness? Or, perhaps, Ling Deqing herself? Or something else again? Was she a mountain that stood in his way? Ever since she had taken him in she had not let him take a nap, or watch television thrillers, or go out, or go to the English Salon and had made him sort rice and do housework. Could it be that he was weary of this kind of life? Was this his "funny kind of freedom"? If not, what was the "funny kind of freedom" that Xiao Zichen wanted?

Again, what was "a river run dry"? Could it be that with the death of Liu Qin the river of Xiao Zichen's love had run dry?

"I really am stupid, truly!" The more Ling Deqing thought about it, the more hurt she felt: "How could I have been so confident as to have believed myself to be a saviour of the world? I rescued Xiao Zichen, but when did he ever care for me?"

"Let him go. I'll have nothing more to do with it." Ling Deqing switched off the light and crept out gently closing the door, leaving it as it was when she arrived. Just as she was turning to go down the stairs she realised that the room was dark and that if Xiao Zichen woke in the night to go to the bathroom, mightn't he trip over? She went back in and turned on the desk lamp on the table for him.

As Ling Deqing crept out again and closed the door there was a sound from the staircase. She turned and looked up, her daughter and son-in-law were standing at the top of the stairs looking at her in wide eyed astonishment: "Aiya! Mother how did you come as well? No wonder nobody answered when we rang home!" Xiao Ying and Wei Wenzhang asked almost in the same breath: "Is dad there?"

After a moment's embarrassment Ling Deqing quickly regained her composure and said: "You've arrived just at the right time, I knew he would come back here, I was just about to ring you. He's asleep. It's up to you!"

Ling Deqing went downstairs by herself. Xiao Ying stopped her mother: "Mother, you've found dad, that's good. You're tired, wait a moment and we'll all go home together." Xiao Ying coaxed her mother back into the apartment.

Xiao Zichen was curled up on the bed peacefully asleep. Xiao Ying shook him: "Dad, dad. Wake up! Wake up!"

Xiao Zichen stirred, mumbled something and carried on sleeping.

"Dad! Dad!" Xiao Ying called again. Xiao Zichen finally opened his eyes a little: "Yingying! You're here, sit down!" Xiao Zichen quickly turned away with something clasped tightly to his chest with both hands.

"Dad, how did you come to be sleeping over here? You've scared us all frantic looking for you. Get up, mother's here as well."

"Mother?" Xiao Zichen instantly opened his eyes wide at the mention of the word, hurriedly looking at Ling Deqing and then at Wei Wenzhang, hands clasped even tighter in front of his chest.

"What's this?" Xiao Ying asked.

Xiao Zichen turned sideways so that Xiao Ying could not touch what he was holding.

Three pairs of eyes were fixed on Xiao Zichen on the bed. Xiao Ying helped her father up: "Dad, it's dark we're going home." As she helped him, Xiao Zichen's hands opened and a white picture frame fell from his grasp on to the bed.

The frame contained a photograph of Liu Qin in a blue dress and white sunhat, standing smiling amidst a garden of red roses. Xiao Ying quickly turned the picture over so that it lay face down on the bed. On the back, prominently written in rough fountain pen characters was:

Oh flower, where are you now?
Oh fruit, I am hidden in your heart!

Quick as she was, Xiao Ying was not quick enough to conceal the frame. She knew that the greatest blow of all was about to descend upon her mother.

Wei Wenzhang quickly slipped out of the room and pretended to be looking out of the window at the night sky.

It took all her strength for Ling Deqing to conceal her feelings, her heart was trembling, she had seen everything. Her lips moved, thinking to say something, but in the end she said nothing and turned on her heel and left the apartment.

"Wenzhang, Wenzhang!" Xiao Ying called hurriedly to her husband. "Quick, take mother home. Take a taxi, she's really tired today."

Despite his extreme reluctance—how could he face his mother-in-law when she had suffered such a blow—Wei Wenzhang had no choice but to follow Ling Deqing downstairs.

Xiao Zichen sat on the edge of the bed in total confusion. Xiao Ying helped him put his shoes on, he felt as if the shoes were on somebody else's feet.

"Dad, if you want to go home to fetch something, you should

tell me so that I can help you. The telephone here has been cut off, how can we get in touch with you? It's really too much!"

Xiao Zichen said without emotion: "Liu Qin told me to come."

Xiao Ying sighed and said: "Dad, Liu Qin's dead!"

"How can that be?" Xiao Zichen could not make it out. "I clearly heard her calling me."

Xiao Zichen had been taking a nap after lunch and had just closed his eyes when he heard "Chen, Chen!" It was Liu Qin calling him. He sat up with a start: "Qin, Qin! Where are you!" He looked around and it seemed that Liu Qin's voice came from the living room. He went into the living room and it seemed that the voice came from the kitchen. In the kitchen, the voice seemed to come from outside the front door. He opened the door and went straight out ...

Xiao Zichen followed Liu Qin's voice out of Pushi Apartments. He flagged down a taxi by Zhapu Road Bridge. The cab driver asked: "Where to, Sir?" He blurted out: "Xiangyang Road!" The cab driver put his foot down and the taxi set off. The noon day roads were empty and they arrived at Xiangyang Road in the twinkling of an eye. In Xiao Zichen's trouser pocket were the 200 yuan that his daughter had given him. He paid the fare, entered the familiar lane, went upstairs to his own apartment on the 5th floor and pushed at the door. He hadn't brought his keys, he stood there in a daze.

Just then, an old neighbor came down the stairs calling him Teacher Xiao: "Teacher Xiao, I haven't seen you for a long time! Have you come back?" In conversation he discovered that Xiao Zichen had no keys and directed him to the locksmith in the lane. Of course, of course, Xiao Zichen quickly went downstairs into the lane, looked around in confusion and found that the locksmith's stall that had been there for years was behind him. It was a small barrow, hung about ding-a-ling with all kinds of keys and bits and pieces. He asked: "Master craftsman, could you give me a hand to open a door? I haven't got the key." The short locksmith looked up at him, this old gentleman seemed familiar, he had seen him before. The locksmith said: "I can't unlock something just like that, there has to be proof of identity, however, I know you, you live here, let's go!" So saying he picked up his tools and followed Xiao Zichen. A couple of turns of a skeleton key in the lock and the door was open. The locksmith told Xiao Zichen: "This lock isn't much good, change it for a better one when you've time." Xiao Zichen paid, the locksmith turned away and Xiao Zichen rushed in without closing the door, saw Liu Qin's funeral portrait and suddenly moist eyed, said with deep emotion: "Qin, I'm back."

Xiao Ying put her father's shoes on and seeing him sitting vacantly there without a word asked: "Dad, what's up?" She waved her hand in front of his eyes and he didn't blink at all. Xiao Ying's heart fell, her father's condition was serious. She was afraid that, in her anger, her mother would refuse to allow him home and urged her father to hurry up. But Xiao Zichen dilly-dallied, muttering that he wanted to go and see Liu Qin, saying that he had been "there".

"There" was Liu Qin's grave at the Peach Blossom Garden cemetery on Xiangzhang Road in Nan Hui. Xiao Zichen had put it in the desk diary, the anniversary of her death outlined in black with "I know you are waiting for me ..." written above.

Her father's undying devotion to Liu Qin caused Xiao Ying considerable grief on her mother's account.

The world was unfair, she felt. There were those with beauty but who lacked attraction and those who were immensely attractive but lacked beauty. Liu Qin was one of these, she had not been at all good looking. She was no longer of this world and yet for her father her attraction remained.

Xiao Ying said in ill humor: "Dad, you are always thinking of Liu Qin, why don't you think of mother? She's broken her heart over you!"

Xiao Zichen said: "But I'm fond of mother as well."

Xiao Ying asked: "Then who do you like best?"

"... I'm fond of one and fonder of the other," said Xiao Zichen earnestly.

Fonder of who? Xiao Ying enquired no further, she knew the answer.

What could be done about anybody's true feelings?

Chapter XIV
Two Ways of Eating Crab Meat Noodles

L ing Deqing sat bolt upright in the taxi on the way home, rather like a figure carved out of white jade.

Wei Wenzhang stole a glance at her in the rear-view mirror and was filled with sympathy. He felt that her spirit was about to break but there was not a trace of it in her face.

Once home, Ling Deqing sent her son-in-law to rest, went into the kitchen and in no time at all made supper. Normally she only eat congee with one or two Suzhou side dishes for supper: pickled eggs, dried salt fish and mustard head in rose syrup. Today, however, because of the time spent looking for Xiao Zichen there had been no time to make congee and she and Wei Wenzhang just had to eat plain boiled rice instead.

"Supper's ready," she called and Wei Wenzhang hurried from his room. As was normal, the food was on the table and the chopsticks laid out. Wei Wenzhang felt particularly guilt-ridden but behaved as if nothing had happened and sat down and eat heartily.

"No time to do anything else today, it's rather simple." Ling Deqing picked up some pickled egg with her chopsticks and placed it in her bowl. Wei Wenzhang distinctly saw that she took a mouthful, chewed for some time and forced herself to swallow.

Wei Wenzhang eat in silence, uncertain of what to say. He thought that of the whole family, it was his mother-in-law who was most to be pitied. She lived for others but they did not live for her; she loved others but they were frightened of her.

Out of the corner of her eye Ling Deqing saw that Wei Wenzhang was secretly observing her and pretending unconcern she said: "I could really do with a bowl of noodle soup!"

Wei Wenzhang quickly said: "We've got noodles, let me help you mother!"

Ling Deqing waved her hand: "What I really want are the Suzhou Zhu Hong Xing restaurant's crab meat noodles, it's autumn, the crabs are plump, it's just the right time."

The Zhu Hong Xing noodle shop? Wei Wenzhang had often heard his mother-in-law mention some of the old Suzhou firms like the Wu Fang Zhai rice dumpling shop and the Huang Tian Yuan pastry shop and of course the Zhu Hong Xing noodle shop as well. But he had never once tried any of them. Even so, they were not all good. Like the Wu Xiang bean shop at the Cheng Huang temple in Shanghai which just fed the nostalgia of the elderly and was not in the least good to eat. He asked Ling Deqing: "Could she make the Zhu Hong Xing's crab meat noodles?"

Ling Deqing's chopsticks picked back and forth in her bowl, smiling she said: "Even if you moved the Zhu Hong Xing's noodle shop to Shanghai and had the same chef, the taste wouldn't be the same."

"A particular place produces a particular kind of person and a particular place produces a particular kind of food. Take water for example, how can the water from the Huangpu in Shanghai compare with the water in Suzhou? Suzhou is near Lake Yangcheng and the rivers and streams enjoy natural advantages."

Wei Wenzhang felt a wave of relief at this topic of conversation. The embarrassment of facing Ling Deqing alone had been dispelled by the Zhu Hong Xing noodle shop. Ling Deqing seemed deeply engaged in the topic and said: "To taste any good, Zhu Hong Xing's noodles have to be eaten on Guanqian Street. Think of it, there's the smell of the rice dumplings from the Wu Fang Zhai wafting across the road and the thick chatter of Suzhou dialect from the cubicles in the restaurant and the big notice in front of the counter which says: 'Crab meat noodles, stewed noodles, eel noodles, stir-fry fish noodles' ... the eye-catching banner at the door: 'Steamed crab meat dumplings on sale!' with a huge exclamation mark which makes it unbearable not to eat. So atmosphere and mood play a large part in whether something is good to eat or not, the actual taste only plays a small part."

Ling Deqing's account had been very detailed. Unless you were a Suzhou gourmet such an account would have been impossible. Wei Wenzhang believed that his mother-in-law's current state of mind of mind was such that even if a bowl of Zhu Hong Xing noodles had been in front of her it would have been tasteless.

Nevertheless, Wei Wenzhang said winningly: "Mother, what you've said makes me want to visit Guanqian Street and eat the original Zhu Hong Xing noodles. When can I go to Suzhou with you?"

"Good, we'll go and eat crab meat noodles, crab meat noodles at the Zhu Hong Xing noodle shop but ..." Ling Deqing said. "The same bowl of crab meat noodles will taste different if eaten differently."

"Eaten differently? You put the noodles in your mouth and that's it," Wei Wenzhang asked curiously. "How can there be two different ways of eating?"

Ling Deqing said: "You don't understand. The Zhu Hong Xing's old way of cooking was to put a piece of crab meat from the opened crab on top of the bowl of crab noodles when it was served. Which do you eat first? Generally, the flavor is in the soup, but the taste of the crab meat conceals any other flavor, how do you eat it so as to get the most satisfaction? One way is to stir the crab meat into the noodles and eat it all together but this weakens the taste of the crab so that you can't taste the actual flavour of the crab meat. That is a very rough way of eating crab noodles. The other way is to carefully pick up a piece of crab together with some noodles, red is red, white is white, yellow is yellow and put them in your mouth bit by bit. When you have finished eating the noodles with the crab you drink some of the soup. You can enjoy the real flavor of the crab meat this way, although the flavour of the noodle soup isn't as good as the crab meat and it's a little weak yet it's just right. This is the gourmet way of eating, different standards of taste and flavor from start to finish!"

Listening to Ling Deqing's discourse on the two ways of eating crab noodles, Wei Wenzhang almost forgot everything that had happened during the afternoon. If people from Suzhou were this particular about eating a bowl of noodles, he thought, then their quality of life was a great deal better than in other places. However, he wondered if Suzhou people were too particular, might not their life be too tiresome? Ling Deqing had suffered a great blow, delivered by her former husband, why give a lecture on the two ways of eating crab noodles?

Whilst Ling Deqing had been enthusiastically discussing the two ways of eating crab meat noodles, Wei Wenzhang had finished the rice in his bowl. The rice in Ling Deqing's bowl had hardly been touched.

Chapter XV
Finality

When supper was over Wei Wenzhang gathered up the bowls and chopsticks, the only domestic chore that the sociologist Wei Wenzhang performed in this household.

The light in Ling Deqing's bedroom was on all night. Wei Wenzhang got up several times and observed the light through a crack in Ling Deqing's bedroom door with deep misgiving, why was she still awake?

This was the night that Ling Deqing made the most momentous decision of her life—to put an end to it.

When she heard the sound of the final person washing in the bathroom cease, she stood up from the sofa where she had been sitting: "My turn now!" She stood on a chair and with some effort brought down a red lacquer box from the top of the wardrobe. It had been part of her dowry on her marriage and had lain there undisturbed for 50 years.

She put the lacquer box in the bath and half filled the bath with water and let it soak.

Next, she took a small brown leather suitcase from the wardrobe and opened it. Inside there were bundle upon bundle of neatly arranged letters, including every letter that she and Xiao

Zichen had exchanged when they were in love before they married. Xiao Zichen's letters had been passionate and unrestrained and had made her heart leap; hers had been graceful and reserved and had not revealed the depth of her feelings. However deep the feeling, she felt it should be conserved drop by drop, squander it and there would be a time when it was exhausted. After they were married, Xiao Zichen had suggested that they should arrange and number all their letters by date, so that when they were old they could read them together; to be able to recollect the past would be a joy. So they had numbered each of these loving letters, a year to a bundle, tied them with green silk ribbon and neatly arranged them in the suitcase.

How could Ling Deqing have known that 30 years later, these passionate words of Xiao Zichen's would, in a different guise, be addressed to another woman?

Very many times had she thought to consign these letters to the flames but in the end had done nothing. They represented her lifetime's greatest treasure, as precious as her very existence itself. The memory of their language, suffused with love, was engraved in her bones and had soon become part of her life.

In the quiet depths of night, when Ling Deqing had been unable to sleep she had sometimes thought of those letters with an aching heart; the idea of until death us do part was just so much nonsense.

At the time of her greatest suffering she had passed the place where Xiao Zichen's and Liu Qin lived, once Route Tenant de la Tour, now Xiangyang Road. She had stealthily glanced at that six story accommodation block. Which figure behind the window had been Xiao Zichen? Could Liu Qin, who could only play the piano and sing, cook him the Suzhou dishes he loved?

Apart from their daughter, these letters were all that remained of the relationship between Ling Deqing and Xiao Zichen, she could not give them up to destruction. Their weighty evidence proved that she had loved and been loved, that she had enjoyed the sweet taste of happiness and that she had also allowed that happiness to someone else. She seemed always to be waiting for something. But waiting for what?

Was it that she had always been waiting for this heartless man to return? Despite Xiao Zichen's regression to childhood she was still confident that her own love could redeem the wayward child that had betrayed her.

Despair is the ultimate limit of hope. Love was the graveyard of Ling Deqing's life.

"I'm stupid, really stupid," Ling Deqing smiled sadly as she looked at the suitcase full of letters. "There has never been a day when I have not felt concern for him, or a time when I have not worried about him or felt that I could change him. This great pile of letters, these fiendish memories, they should have been cleaned out and utterly destroyed long ago!"

In the bath the cracks in the dried out lacquer box had swollen in the water and no longer leaked. Ling Deqing put the suitcase on the edge of the bath, locked the bathroom door and sat down on a chair.

Only two things were needed now, matches and a spirit lamp, she could then finally do away with her past ill-fated relationship with Xiao Zichen.

This very much resembled a farewell ceremony in which she bade farewell to the only love of her life.

She went through the letters, not wanting to look but unable not to. The designs that represented the mood of the moment: a plum blossom, a little bird, a green leaf, and open book, a red apple, were all masterpieces of the time. In each letter the salutation "Qing" or "Zichen" was redolent of sweetness and warmth.

Qing,
I tossed and turned and couldn't get to sleep. I thank God that the tearful me discovered the gentle you. You are no more an illusion and I no longer cling to a delusion. You are before me, as if the spirit of love had suddenly appeared and cleared the tears from my

eyes. Your serene gaze has dissolved my despair and this
weeping boy has gained new life ...

This letter, marked No.1, had long been engraved on Ling
Deqing's heart. It had been written, one stormy rain drenched
night, by the lovelorn, despairing Xiao Zichen the moment he
returned to his St. John's University dormitory from the tender
embrace of Ling Deqing that had given him new life.

Ling Deqing determinedly struck a match and lit the spirit
lamp. She was slightly dazzled by the blue flame and the match
burned down to her finger before she dropped it into the box with
a hiss, leaving a tendril of blue smoke. Her hand was shaking and
the letter trembled, the flame danced and she heard the thump of
her heart beating. She hesitated a moment as the paper of the letter
approached the flame. She could recite each weighted word of this
letter and even if turned to ash it would remain in her heart.

The letter caught fire, burst into flame in an instant and
then turned to a black ash that floated in the air around the bath.

One letter followed another and the ash floating in the box
became blacker and blacker. Ling Deqing poured the blackened
water into the lavatory and it gurgled into the drains as she
flushed it away time after time.

Suddenly, she felt that these boxfuls of black water were like
Meng Po's tea of forgetfulness in Chinese opera.

The bathroom was filled with the smell of smoke and burning
that penetrated the door cracks to her bedroom. How long she
had been burning she did not know but the brown suitcase was
empty and her legs had lost all feeling.

That was it. Done with. Ling Deqing put the suitcase back
in the wardrobe. She opened the bedroom window and a cool
breeze flowed in, she took a deep breath. That weighty business
had been lightly disposed of.

The Zen principle of "casting away" was that simple.

Ling Deqing looked out of the window, a glimmer of light
appeared on the overcast horizon, she felt utterly relaxed.

Chapter XVI
Last Testament

Ling Deqing took out a black notebook, she was going to render an account of her life.

Her head was swimming and she patted her forehead, she was tired. It didn't matter, once she had written what she wanted to say she would have a bath and a good sleep. Even if heaven and earth were to split asunder tomorrow, she would be free of the anxieties of this life.

She took up her pen, it felt heavy. There was much to say that had long lain dormant in her mind.

Yingying, my child,
During the course of my life at the hospital I have seen too much of life and death. But how can one understand death without knowing life? Death is not necessarily tragic nor life necessarily a joy. The crux is one's attitude to life.

For a body that suffers unbearably, death is full of love; for the old who can no longer summon up the strength, it is a kind of blessing. The ancients called death "a return", this is very apt. "Return" means going home. The territory of life is merely a way-station, true home is where one came from. Birth is to set out on a long journey and death is to return home.

When a person knows contentment it is time to go home and not to linger. We live in this world, weak in strength and perhaps may see no achievement in our lives, but there is a world in each flower and heaven in every grain of sand.

I know contentment. As he lay dying, Li Shutong[1] wrote the words "At the crossing point of the departure from the suffering of this world and the joy of paradise". This is a portrayal of life and the completed life is always like this.

I am old. I am not sad at the frailty of my body, what I fear is that through its frailty I will lose the ability to be in command.

If, in the midst of unforeseen change, there comes a day when through the onset of illness I lose my grip on life and I become useless and a burden upon you, I beseech you, my daughter Yingying, if you truly love me, to help me die. All you need to do is to dissolve the dose you will find in the phial in my red dressing box in water and let me drink it. This is my last gift to myself and the best present that you, my most beloved daughter, can give your mother.

Abandoning a body that suffers unbearably through euthanasia accords with morality.

I absolutely realise that the law does not permit this and I write this testament in black and white to seek forgiveness for my daughter who loves me.

After my death I wish my cornea to be donated to someone who needs sight and my body to be donated to

---

1   Li Shutong (1880–1942), Buddhist monk, musician, painter, calligrapher and teacher.—*Trans.*

the Shanghai Medical College.

If through departing this life I cannot write further, what I have written here today stands as my testament.

Ling Deqing

Ling Deqing knew in her heart that however capable a person was, there would come a day when they would be incapable. She wished to take her daughter's hand and rely on her help to finish life's final journey. Ling Deqing was more intelligent than most and with almost supernatural foresight but had she thought whether or not her filial daughter would really obey her?

But there was no other route for Ling Deqing the hospital matron. She had already previously raised the question of donating her body with her daughter who had been strenuously opposed to the idea. Her daughter had hoped that her precious body would not be donated to dissected by others, it utterly lacked dignity. Ling Deqing failed to comprehend, there had never been any lack of bodies donated for dissection when she had been at medical college, why was it that over the last fifty years or so people had become more and more petty minded and were unwilling to donate their bodies? In the past she had taught her daughter that true dignity did not lie in whether or not one's body was complete but in nobility of spirit. The greatest shame of all was loss of morality and meanness of character. Do you think that dignity comes with clothing? Or that the unclothed body is shameful? After death one is freed from care, the body cannot remain, only one's character remains with the world! Donating my body is the greatest dignity of all.

Having written all this, Ling Deqing wondered whether her daughter, who had so opposed the donation of her body, would assist her in euthanasia.

Ling Deqing had never before written so much to her daughter and she was tired. The cool breeze that blew through the window ruffled her white hair. Her heart started to beat irregularly and she clutched at her chest, it was time to rest.

Dawn was breaking, Ling Deqing closed the window and drew the dark green velvet curtains. She half-filled the bath with water and had a comfortable bath. People from Suzhou called having a bath, *huoyu*—splashing water, she thought the imagery particularly appropriate. After her bath she put on a white toweling bathrobe and felt much warmer.

Ling Deqing went into the bedroom, the swish swish sound of street cleaning came through the window, another dark night had passed and a new day had started.

Ling Deqing turned towards her bed, she was suddenly dizzy, swayed a little and then collapsed gently at the foot of the bed.

At the moment of collapse she was absolutely clear-headed and was thinking: "Today is a day of complete renewal and I have no more cares."

Chapter XVII
Beware of the Gas

Ling Deqing had had a stroke, a cerebral occlusion. She was rushed to hospital and was unconscious for three days and nights but eventually regained consciousness.

Xiao Ying stayed with her for those three days but developed a fever on the night of the fourth day, so that her whole body seemed to boil. A sympathetic hospital worker urged her to go home and rest.

In the chill of a Shanghai early autumn morning Xiao Ying dragged her exhausted body through the entrance to Pushi Apartments and a whiff of old fashioned cooking oil and damp assailed her nostrils, she felt very unwell.

Ever since the 50s, due to an expanding population and a pressing lack of housing many people in the Pushi Apartments had moved their kitchens into the corridors. Xiao Ying took the lift and made her way past the pots and pans and kitchen stoves, smelt the odor of fish and felt nauseated. She looked up and saw a dried eel hanging overhead, quickening her step through the hanging washing she arrived at her own front door.

Opening the door, she stumbled through the kitchen into the living room, the apartment was silent. She carefully opened the door to her bedroom, Wei Wenzhang was sleeping soundly with his back to her.

Xiao Ying fell on to the bed with a bump.

Wei Wenzhang woke and with eyes filled with pleasant surprise gently asked: "Ying, you're back, you must be tired, how's your mother? I'll get you something to eat …"

Xiao Ying, eyes closed covered her mouth, she felt like being sick, the power of speech had left her. She pointed to her head, it ached! Wei Wenzhang stretched out a hand to feel it, it was burning hot. He quickly got up, took off her dress and shoes and covered her with the quilt. "Do you want to see a doctor? Why didn't you see a doctor in the emergency department at the hospital when you were there?" Xiao Ying had been to the emergency department at the hospital before she left and had seen the duty doctor slumped over the desk fast asleep and had not had the heart to wake him. On reflection, he was tired from night duty, there was medicine at home and so she had come home. At the moment, all she could think of was sleep, a deep sleep. Wei Wenzhang found an antipyretic in the drawer and got her to swallow it. She was soon asleep. Wei Wenzhang saw that it was only 4 a.m. and went back to sleep.

Xiao Ying had a disturbed night and did not sleep properly, she dreamed uneasily on and on. One moment it was her mother chasing her and the next moment her father. She did not know why she had to escape, to flee for her life but she was caught, caught by whom? Then there was a searchlight but why? Suddenly the dreamscape changed. Whoever had caught her felt her face, she reached out to push them away but couldn't raise her hands. "Wenzhang?!" she was angry. "What are you up to, I'm ill." She shouted and woke herself up, dazzled by the light in her eyes. Her father was standing there, shining a torch in her face.

"Dad! What are you doing?" she said, sitting up in alarm. She couldn't open her eyes and shielded them from the light with her hands: "Dad, what are you doing, coming in here so early?"

Xiao Zichen looked lovingly at his daughter and said

reproachfully: "Yingying, where have you been these last few days, and where's mother got to as well?"

"Shh!" Xiao Ying looked at her soundly sleeping husband and put her finger to her lips. "Dad, not so loud, let me sleep a bit could you? If there's anything to say it can wait until tomorrow, I'm really tired!"

"Fine, fine, it's good you're back!" Xiao Zichen turned on his heel and quietly left the room.

As her father had first opened and then closed the door Xiao Ying had faintly noticed the smell of burning as it drifted in from outside, what was it? She wrinkled her nose and sniffed, leaped from the bed and rushed into the kitchen. Their conversation had already woken Wei Wenzhang who on hearing his wife mention the smell of burning followed her in to the kitchen.

The gas on the stove was turned up under a stainless steel pan. Removing the lid revealed a mess of burnt congee, the white rice scorched to a yellow porridge with the smell of burning rising from the bottom of the pan.

In a flurry of hands and feet, Xiao Ying and Wei Wenzhang abandoned all thought of sleep. The window was opened, the stove cleaned and the pan put to soak in water. Xiao Ying had just taken some medicine, her headache had retreated a little and she was more awake. Xiao Zichen stood there, embarrassed and looking rather frightened.

Xiao Ying and her husband sighed as they rushed about. Neither wanted to blame Xiao Zichen and just said: "Dad, you can't manage turning on the gas, why did you turn it on?"

Xiao Zichen could not remember going into the kitchen or having burnt the congee. He vaguely remembered that he had been dreaming and that Liu Qin had come, her face alight with smiles, he had been happy and was just going to greet her when she disappeared. He sat up thinking to go after her when he heard footsteps in the living room. He crept out to look and saw through a crack that his daughter had returned. He hadn't seen her for several days and was delighted, Yingying's back! But she went into her bedroom and closed the door.

Xiao Zichen thought that as mother wasn't here there was nobody to cook. His daughter would be hungry and he was rather hungry himself, who was to cook? He didn't remember what he did next. He wanted to tell his daughter to get up and eat and was standing in front of her bed but the room was very dark. He went and got a torch from his own room, shone it and saw that his daughter's face was completely red and that she was snoring gently. He stroked her face, nice and warm, he was overjoyed!

Xiao Zichen went back to his room and sat disconsolately on the edge of the bed. "When did I turn on the gas?" He made an effort to gather up the shards and fragments of memory but none of them contained any detail of going in to the kitchen. Xiao Zichen was dejected: "How could I have done it!" He struck his head with his fist in utter despondency.

As they cleaned the pan Xiao Ying and Wenzhang said anxiously that the old fashioned gas stove was really unsafe and should be fitted with an extinguishing mechanism, everybody else had them fitted. "The last time Dad burnt a pan, mother said she would ask you to get one, did you forget?"

"I didn't forget," said Wei Wenzhang as he cleaned the stove. "I was going to buy a new stove, this one is pre-1949 liberation and is really too old, the new ones have extinguishers fitted, I'll buy one the moment I have time."

"Good," said Xiao Ying. "It looks as if I shall have to quickly find a housekeeper."

Wei Wenzhang said nothing. Whilst his mother-in-law was in hospital and they were at work and the housekeeper was alone with Xiao Zichen, there would bound to be problems. He thought that inaction trumped action and it would be best to leave things as they were.

Seeing that her husband said nothing, Xiao Ying ventured: "Otherwise we can see if we can find a suitable old people's home on the internet, see which is best and then make the time to go and look at it."

This matched Wei Wenzhang's inclination. Wei Wenzhang the sociologist had always advocated the principle that society should help the old. That the elderly should go into old people's homes was an inevitable concomitant of an ageing society and the direction in which society itself was moving. However, he knew that his wife could not bear to see her father put in an old people's home and said: "Think about it and see whether dad agrees or not." Of course, Xiao Ying had not the heart to put her father into a home but if she considered her mother she could not consider her father nor even take account of her own health. Ai!

Backwards and forwards in this way dawn arrived. Xiao Ying's fever had receded a little. She quickly made breakfast, hot milk, toast and fried eggs. Wei Wenzhang wanted his wife to rest but she was unwilling and intended to talk to her father. She knew that her father liked sandwiches. She buttered two pieces of toast, added jam, placed them together, cut them across diagonally and put them in a shallow blue dish. She was practiced in all this and made her father's breakfast exactly the same way as her mother did.

"Dad! Come and have breakfast," called Xiao Ying as she put a mug of steaming milk, two triangular toast and jam sandwiches, a yellow and white fried egg and a glass of orange juice on the table.

Xiao Zichen was hiding in his room, stunned at having burnt the congee. He quickly emerged the moment his daughter called. He looked at his breakfast with delight. His son-in-law had made his breakfast for the last few days, the bread had not been toasted and the sandwiches had not been cut diagonally. Xiao Zichen felt that un-toasted bread did not taste the same and that it was slightly more civilized to eat sandwiches that had been cut diagonally. It was no wonder, Wei Wenzhang came from a worker's family and had grown up eating rice soup, form meant nothing to him. His daughter Xiao Ying understood her father, he had once told her that this way of cutting sandwiches was the embodiment of civilization and good breeding.

"Dad, drink it while it's hot," said Xiao Ying as she added a spoonful of coffee to the milk. Xiao Zichen liked drinking this kind of coffee. He said that adding milk to coffee was the European way of drinking it and that adding coffee to milk was the American Rhode Island way of drinking it. Xiao Ying had recently read in a medical magazine at the library that coffee helped prevent and delay dementia and had urged her father to drink it.

"I was really hungry early on!" Xiao Zichen eat his sandwiches and enjoyed the coffee. Xiao Ying thought to herself that her father must definitely have been hungry early in the morning before going in to the kitchen and making rice soup. She really ought to buy some snacks for him. She asked: "Dad, what were you doing, going and making congee?"

Xiao Zichen shook his head: "I don't remember."

Xiao Ying asked: "But you don't like rice soup!"

Xiao Zichen said earnestly: "Mother likes rice soup."

Xiao Ying's heart was moved. Her father must believe that her mother was back home. She had hated her father when she had been at the hospital, he had caused her mother's stroke but the hatred had dissolved on hearing her father's remark about making rice soup for her mother. She tidied her father's collar and said that mother couldn't come home at the moment, she would be in hospital for a while.

Xiao Zichen said that after breakfast he wanted to go and see her. Not possible. Xiao Ying urged that it would be better to wait until she was a little better.

Xiao Zichen was being particularly well-behaved today and nodded obediently in agreement.

Xiao Ying asked him: "Dad, mother's ill in hospital and there's nobody at home to look after you. Wenzhang has to go to work, we are thinking of something for you."

Xiao Zichen said: "I'll be good, I won't go out."

"Dad, would you be willing to stay in an old people's home for a few days until mother's better?"

Xiao Zichen asked in alarm: "Old people's home? What sort of place is that?"

"An old people's home," said Xiao Ying, "has a lot of old people there who eat together, sleep and chat, play games and can do exercises."

"Will you be there?"

"I won't be there, I have to see mother in hospital and go to work."

"Then I won't go either," Xiao Zichen said resolutely.

"Why not? There are a lot of people there."

"I don't know them."

"You may not know them to begin with but you'll gradually get to know them."

"I won't go!" Xiao Zichen said stubbornly.

Xiao Ying was very patient and said: "Dad, go and try, if you're not happy then come back. We really worry about you if we're not at home."

Xiao Zichen put down his toast, looked imploringly at Xiao Ying and said: "Yingying, I won't put on the gas, I promise I won't put on the gas!"

Seeing her father's imploring look, Xiao Ying's heart softened. She had been hesitant about this to start with and did not persevere in the face of her father's unwillingness.

Wei Wenzhang had quietly listened to the conversation between the two from the sideline. He had hoped that his wife's attitude would have been a little more resolute. He hadn't realized that she had no intention of persuading her father to go. Seeing his wife give up, he couldn't help interjecting: "Dad, the mother of a colleague mine went to live in an old people's home and although she was unhappy to start with, she discovered when she was there that she was much happier than at home. Lots of people together, not lonely like at home, really lively and she made some new friends."

"Then you go!" Xiao Zichen looked not at his son-in-law but at the cups, dishes and coffee jug on the table as he enunciated word by word and phrase by phrase: "One plus one, add one, equals nought."

Wei Wenzhang and Xiao Ying were dumbfounded and looked at each other as they pondered her father's meaning. From time to time Xiao Zichen came out with a phrase that everybody was at a loss to understand. When you looked at it in detail however, it usually had some connection with what was currently going on. What he wished to express was not nonsense.

Xiao Ying guessed that what her father meant was that although the old people's home contained many people, one plus one add one, as far as Xiao Zichen was concerned it was of no significance, equals nought. Because he knew nobody at all. Wei Wenzhang surmised that "one plus one, add one, equals nought" referred to Xiao Ying and himself, and, adding to the example, three together still could not persuade Xiao Zichen, equals nought.

Xiao Ying fetched a sheet of white typing paper and a marker pen from the desk and wrote in large clear characters:

"DAD, DON'T TURN ON THE GAS!"

She then stuck it on the top of the stove with transparent sticky tape, saying as she did so: "Dad, you mustn't be angry, this is for your own good, you mustn't turn on the gas unless somebody lets you, it's dangerous."

"Yes, yes!" Xiao Zichen, seeing that his daughter was no longer talking of the old people's home, was delighted. He cocked his head on one side and looked at the strip of paper nodding: "Dad, that's me," pointing to himself, "I'm Xiao Zichen, that's to say Xiao Zichen mustn't turn on the gas, right?"

Xiao Ying nodded, correct, however, she had another thought and wrote a further strip amending "Dad" to "Xiao Zichen" so that it read "Xiao Zichen must not turn on the gas", this was much more to the point, her father would be less likely to make a mistake.

Xiao Ying stuck up the strip and Xiao Zichen patted it saying: "Excellent, excellent, really firm." On the way back to his room he mumbled to himself: "I'm Xiao Zichen, Xiao Zichen mustn't turn on the gas ..."

Chapter XVIII
Death Is Difficult

Ling Deqing was eventually discharged from hospital and returned home. She was paralysed down one side.

As she lay in bed in her room her eyes moved inch by inch. She carefully savored everything that she could see from her bed, the peeling white ceiling, the old fashioned cream colored chandelier and the light green walls. The light brown sofa, the maroon high-backed chair, the dark brown desk, the dark green curtains, the old-fashioned brown wall clock ... From the depths of her memory she could recall every book in the bookcase, every handicraft piece, where they had come from, who had bought them and how long they had been there.

Ling Deqing knew this room, it had been with her whole life and every object in it was alive and seemed like a member of her family. When she concentrated her gaze on them, she could speak with them and tell them her innermost thoughts.

She had bought the copy of Florence Nightingale's *Notes on Nursing* that was in the bookcase when she had been studying at the Women's Medical College. She had read it she did not know how many times. That spot on the wall had been made one hot summer when Wei Le, helping her get rid of mosquitoes, had swatted one, leaving a speck of blood. He had said: "You are not to annoy granny, you are to be re-born in the next life as a beneficial insect, do you hear?" Ling Deqing started to smile to herself as she recalled how sweet Wei Le had been.

Ling Deqing fixed her eyes on the large citrus-wood wardrobe, her gaze penetrating its door and coming to rest on the rosewood dressing case containing her last testament in the drawer. When she had recovered consciousness in hospital and she had thought she was about to leave this world she had congratulated herself on having written it that dark night. She had wanted her daughter to go home and read it. But over the last few days Yingying had made no response at all.

Had Yingying read it and was pretending that she had not or had she been so busy that she hadn't had the time?

The dressing case in the drawer, so close, but she was semi-paralyzed and she lacked the strength to reach it. One reached this state of helplessness, she could do nothing without the help of others. All that was left to her was the ability to swallow, with difficulty to move her hands and feet and to speak in a mumble. Beyond that was the ability to empty her bowels. What distinguished this kind of person from the dead? What use was she? Ling Deqing knitted her brows in suffering.

Everybody wanted to live and as far as other people were concerned emerging from hospital alive was a miracle. As far as Ling Deqing was concerned however, living like this was a catastrophe. The quality and dignity of life was much more important than prolonging it. In order to avoid adding to her daughter's troubles she wanted to cast off and to abandon treatment. Nobody at the hospital had understood her. The doctors, nurses and nursing assistants had only considered themselves and whether they might be held responsible. She had tried to pull out the tubes but the nursing assistants had tied her wrists down. Yang Feiyan, the pretty nursing assistant had tricked her and coaxed her and had even held her hand tightly throughout one sleepless night.

Ling Deqing had hovered between life and death for several days, and had set foot on the Bridge of No Return. She had drunk Meng Po's potion of forgetfulness and thought that her troubles were over only to regain consciousness and to discover that although her heart had been destroyed her memory had not. She had forgotten nothing and remembered everything.

Death was difficult, as difficult as this.

Fate had tossed her on to the bed with a bladder catheter and bag. As she lay there Ling Deqing realized that there really was a limit to the strength of the individual, life had its own natural rules and as she took life's final steps she slowly waited for death.

Perhaps it was as well. She had had no great wish to return home alive but had done so and was content that she had been able to be together with her family and enjoy its happiness. Nevertheless, lying in bed like this would be unendurable if she could not get up to help her daughter through the crisis of Xiao Zichen's illness or to cook for Wei Le.

Ling Deqing calmly examined every object in the room and recalled event after event from the past. These objects were engraved with happiness and with suffering. The passage of time had dimmed the happiness and tears had diluted the suffering. Unconsciously, the joy and suffering reached the deepest recesses of her heart and lived there peacefully for days, neither knowing nor feeling. Gradually, her life in space-time was running out, its future short, leaving behind limitless memories.

When only memories are left, life is more or less finished. But the very existence of memory indicated that she was still alive.

Some memories, because of the passing of life, no longer exist; others form the precious history of the ages, they are like fossils.

Looking at the furnishings in the room and thinking of the events of the past, Ling Deqing closed her eyes in bewilderment and dream after dream with neither beginning nor end swirled through her head.

She was floating in space looking down on herself lying in

the bed, she conversed with her dream self.

The Ling Deqing on the bed asked: "I don't want to be a burden on others, what should I do?"

The Ling Deqing in space replied: "Coming together is parting, in life there is nothing that does not die."

The Ling Deqing in the bed said: "I understand, yet don't understand ..."

At some point, there was somebody else next to her, a strange young woman. Huh, it must be the new housekeeper that her daughter had found, with a head of black hair that half-covered her face, lying curled up asleep next to her and snoring all night.

Time and again Xiao Ying came in during the night and try as she might was unable to wake the girl. Xiao Ying could only help her mother herself, turning her over and patting her back. Looking at her daughter's weary face in the dim light from the wall lamp Ling Deqing felt guilty, she didn't go back to sleep and remained with her eyes open until dawn.

The sun rose and Ling Deqing welcomed another day. In the morning, a nurse from the district hospital came to sterilize her bladder catheter and Ling Deqing started to become irritable. This hateful tube advertised the utter lack of quality and dignity of her life. She would rather her dead naked body became a textbook to be read in detail by students in the dissecting room than live dragging this sort of tail around. With a tail like this she couldn't even wear pants to protect her modesty. Before she left hospital the doctors had withdrawn the catheter and she had been overjoyed. But for a whole day retention of urine had left her in agony, she had lost the ability to pass water by herself. They had had to re-insert the catheter and she had immediately passed 2,500 c.c. of urine and had nearly fainted.

The body's exits were actually like the exits of a river, silting up and flood could both lead to mortal danger. Helplessly she accepted the tube and the cruel reality. This tiny physiological sluice gate, to be operated by others, to be opened and closed several times a day until she left this world.

No, No! She struggled and tried to pull out the catheter. Xiao Ying restrained her. The strength in Ling Deqing's arms was now much greater than when she had been in hospital and she kept on saying: "Out, pull it out!" She would rather die from retention of urine than live dragging this tail. "Mother, you can't do this, you can't do it!" Xiao Ying said, reduced to tears. The nurse looked on baffled: "What's up with your mother? If she pulls it out and can't pass water, she'll have to go back to hospital to have it re-inserted and that'll be a nuisance for her and a nuisance for all of you too!"

As expected Ling Deqing quietened down when she heard this. Yes, going to hospital and making more trouble for her daughter, that was something she did not wish.

Ai, dying was so difficult!

Ling Deqing did not know how much further she had to travel on this final stretch of road. How much more trouble could she cause her family? There was already Xiao Zichen, and then add a bed-ridden her. Ai, these days!

In her old age and in the sleepless quiet of night she had, times without number, thought of various ways of dying. She had seen too much death during her work as a nurse. Some tormented by pain between life and death had sought death but had not been granted it; some had peacefully ceased breathing in their dreams and passed in tranquility. Birth was purely a matter of chance but death was a certainty. Nobody could determine their own final journey. Ling Deqing wanted, above all, to depart the world in her sleep or simply to drop dead without fuss. She had prepared sufficiently for this but nobody can choose the manner of their death beforehand except through suicide. In her present state, Ling Deqing did not even have the possibility of suicide. She was like a fettered criminal utterly without the strength to resist. All the plans that she had made in the past had become totally useless.

One method was left to Ling Deqing, to refuse medication. This was one of her remaining abilities. The housekeeper Little Jiang, the girl who had slept so heavily that night brought boiled warm water and put the medication, pill by pill, in the palm of her hand, but urge as she might, Ling Deqing kept her mouth tightly closed.

Little Jiang gave her a look, turned away and thought up another method. She crushed the pills, dissolved them in water and gave it to Ling Deqing to drink. The moment Ling Deqing tasted the bitter flavor she spat it back into the cup.

Little Jiang then mixed the medication into food but the moment she tasted it Ling Deqing frowned and again spat it out.

Xiao Ying was deeply hurt when she heard Little Jiang complain that her mother would not take her medication. Her mother was clearly improving day by day, why should she want to let go? She knew her mother, unwilling to impose on others but mother, mother, you have given so much for us, why won't you let us give a little back to you? Why won't you let us do this for you as is right and proper?

Little Jiang lost patience, her voice rising when Xiao Ying and Wei Wenzhang were not present: "Huh! Old Ancestor, you won't take your medication and pull out your bladder tube, you're impatient with life is that it? Let me tell you, we country people have no medicine even when we want it. We have no hospital to go to even if we wanted to. What's wrong with the good conditions you have here? What's it matter to me if you don't take your medication? I don't want to carry on anyway, I'm off tomorrow and you can wet and shit yourself all you like, so you stink so much people won't come near you and see how many days you can stand that!"

Ling Deqing was taken aback at being abused by Little Jiang. Nobody had been so fiercely unpleasant to her in her whole life. What was it with this girl? Even Ling Deqing, who had no fear of death had been scared to a standstill by what she said. If Little Jiang really went off in a huff, her daughter would have to take care of her bodily functions. If there were nobody to clean her up the smell would be unbearable even to herself.

She thought: if I am to die, I want to die clean and with a little dignity. She then decided to follow instructions.

Chapter XIX
Little Jiang the Housekeeper

On the fifth day that she was with Ling Deqing, Little Jiang the housekeeper chilled Xiao Ying's heart.

The first night, Little Jiang fell asleep beside Ling Deqing, slept heavily until dawn and could not be woken. Xiao Ying got up twice during the night and went to look at her mother, the little electronic alarm clock on the bedside table was flashing away, beep-beep, beep-beep and Little Jiang lay wrapped in the quilt without stirring a hair.

But Ling Deqing had woken and eyes wide open, was staring terrified at the strange girl beside her. Xiao Ying switched on the light, called to her mother and then looked at Little Jiang, her sleeping shape induced pity. She shook Little Jiang who turned over impatiently, licked her lips, mumbled something and went back to sleep. Xiao Ying thought: perhaps she's too tired, let her sleep well, it may not work the first night but it will slowly get better.

Xiao Ying helped her mother empty her bladder and patted her back but her mother was heavy and she couldn't turn her over. Ling Deqing tried hard to move herself but could not find the strength and was filled with remorse for her daughter.

The second night when Xiao Ying went to look at her mother, the alarm clock was ringing at the right time, her mother moved and Little Jiang was sound asleep. Xiao Ying thought now is not the time to be soft-hearted and shook Little Jiang. "Little Jiang, Little Jiang, get up, it's time to turn grandma over!" She called a dozen times and at last Little Jiang moved slightly and squint-eyed mumbled: "You tire me to death!"

Full of apologies Xiao Ying said: "I'm really sorry, Little Jiang, grandma has to be turned over twice during the night otherwise she'll get bedsores, her bladder has to be emptied as well, I thought we agreed ..."

"I know!" Little Jiang sat up indolently, pouting as she shuffled into her slippers and moved to Ling Deqing's bedside, roughly lifting her and turning her over. Her strength was considerable and hurt Ling Deqing who emitted a soft moan. Xiao Ying was distressed. Next Little Jiang slapped Ling Deqing's back so hard that Ling Deqing groaned aloud with pain. Xiao Ying's heart ached again. She wanted to tell Little Jiang to be gentle but was frightened of upsetting her. She could only suffer in silence.

Little Jiang returned to the other side of the bed, lay down and went to sleep. Xiao Ying woke her: "There's still emptying her bladder and flushing it away!" Little Jiang pouting, had to get up and do it. The look on her face showed that Xiao Ying was obviously doing this to spite her and the rough handling had been a silent protest.

Xiao Ying did not sleep well for the next two nights. The third night she was exhausted and frightened that if she went to sleep she wouldn't wake. She put an alarm clock next to her pillow. The alarm clock went off and woke Wei Wenzhang. Wei Wenzhang complained: "Don't we have Little Jiang? Are you still worried?" Feeling guilty on her husband's account Xiao Ying quickly turned off the alarm.

Xiao Ying went in to her mother where the alarm clock had just started to ring but shake Little Jiang as she might, she remained fast asleep and would not wake. Xiao Ying sighed and had to turn her mother over, pat her back and empty her bladder. She was doing what Little Jiang should be doing. Distressed for love of her daughter, Ling Deqing stretched out the hand that was not paralyzed, stroked her daughter's face and sighed.

Xiao Ying went back to bed but could not sleep. Wei Wenzhang had also been woken and the two of them were helpless and bleary eyed. The intention had been that Little Jiang should help them, instead it turned out that Xiao Ying was helping Little Jiang. Wei Wenzhang blamed his wife for being too soft-hearted, there should be some rules for a housekeeper. Xiao Ying, on the other hand, feared being too strict, upsetting Little Jiang and hardening her attitude to her mother. Most of all she was frightened that she would leave in a huff. Truth to tell, finding a housekeeper was no easy matter.

"Yang Feiyan, the nursing assistant at the hospital was good," Xiao Ying couldn't help saying. "She was capable and responsible." Wei Wenzhang uttered not a word. After a while, up spoke Wei Wenzhang the sociologist: "Even the best have to be managed, management is a science, even if it's just one person you have to learn how to manage." Xiao Ying mocked her husband: "You really can teach the theory."

On the morning of the fourth day, Xiao Ying thought that she would have a good talk with Little Jiang. It was another night without proper sleep and when she got up she was dizzy and her head ached. Little Jiang, however, was happily humming away in the kitchen. She had been to the vegetable market early and brought back breakfast and vegetables and had noisily rung the doorbell. Xiao Ying rushed to open the door wondering: didn't I give her a key, why can't she open it herself? All Xiao Ying could do was to go and open the door for her.

Little Jiang washed and sorted vegetables in the kitchen. Xaio Ying asked: "What are you singing?"

Little Jiang said: "The first one was Tao Zhe's *Love Me or Love Him* and the other was Zhang Hanyun's *If You Want to Sing Then Sing*, what do you think Aunt Xiao, do you like them?" She hummed them again: "We didn't speak in the dark, you want to go home I don't want you to go, loneliness deep as the sea is frightening, your soft hand gently strokes my hair ..."

Xiao Ying had not the heart to listen to these boring songs but politely said: "I'm afraid I don't understand these to and fro love songs." Little Jiang made a face: "Doesn't that doorbell of yours have a to and fro love song? 'Wait a minute, or a minute more, I can feel your heartache too, I won't let parting be for ever'." Little Jiang hummed the doorbell's tune. Xiao Ying said: "My son likes it and put it on the doorbell."

Little Jiang said: "That song's really good, I loved the bell the moment I came through the door!"

At this point Xiao Ying realized why Little Jiang hadn't use her key, she had wanted to ring the bell.

Taking advantage of Little Jiang's good mood, Xiao Ying summoned up the courage to ask: "Little Jiang, is that alarm clock in the room not loud enough at night, can't you hear it?"

Little Jiang said: "I can hear it but I can't wake up!"

Xiao Ying sighed: "Slowly does it, you'll get used to it."

Little Jiang said: "I'm not used to getting up in the middle of the night."

Xiao Ying was very sympathetic: "If you can't sleep well because you're getting up in the middle of the night, if there's nothing to do you can take a nap in the afternoon."

Little Jiang said: "Sleeping during the day, what a pity! I've never slept during the day," and went on humming her song, "why can't those in love be together, why ..."

Xiao Ying had other things to say but seeing that Little Jiang was intoxicated with the sound of her songs and was washing vegetables under the tap swaying to the music, she swallowed her words. Never mind, talk again when I get back from work.

In the evening, Xiao Ying came back from work to find the table spread with dishes of chicken, duck, fish and bean curd but without a single vegetable dish. Xiao Ying had told Little Jiang time and again to prepare a vegetable dish, perhaps she didn't like vegetables. Never mind, mix them up, Xiao Ying tasted it, it could hardly be called good. Xiao Ying thought that too much should not be asked of Little Jiang. As long as she was positive, let her do the shopping, let her cook, things would improve slowly. Xiao Ying went into her mother's room. Little Jiang was feeding her, spoonful by spoonful, very patiently it seemed. With much effort her mother was eating, mouthful by mouthful.

Xiao Ying came out thinking: "We can get by like this."

But that night, the same as ever, Little Jiang wouldn't get up so that Xiao Ying was even more exhausted than she had been sitting through the nights in hospital. Her myocarditis had not got better and as soon as she got up in the night her heart beat became irregular, each time feeling as if her heart would jump out of her mouth, painful at every beat.

On the morning of the fifth day, with great forbearance Xiao Ying asked pleasantly: "Little Jiang, do you remember the requirements I discussed with you at the domestic agency?" Little Jiang nodded: "Yes!" She was chewing mouthfuls of a meat bun that she had just bought and drinking soy milk from a cup. Xiao Ying said: "I told you that you would have to get up twice during the night but you haven't got up even once!"

Little Jiang swallowed her mouthful of bun and asked: "Well, what are you going to do about it?"

Xiao Ying said: "You agreed to our conditions. Do you think that you have met them or not?"

Little Jiang wiped her mouth: "What would you say?"

Xiao Ying said with a smile: "I'm asking you!"

Little Jiang said: "If you think I'll do then that's OK, if you don't, then it isn't and it's letting me go isn't it?"

Xiao Ying was stupefied, it looked as if she didn't want to continue working, what could you ask of a housekeeper who didn't want to carry on? Xiao Ying withdrew her smile and said: "If you can't get up in the night, then I shall have to consider other arrangements."

"Right!" Little Jiang was very blunt. She calmly finished her breakfast and then went and packed her belongings. She dawdled for hours in the bathroom washing her hair, having a bath and making up. When she emerged she gave Xiao Ying a fright, the smell of scent assailed her nostrils and the sight dazzled her eyes, rather like a young miss from entertainment city.

"Do you want to search my bag?" Little Jiang, face full of disdain, pushed her wheeled suitcase towards Xiao Ying.

"No, no," said Xiao Ying hurriedly, "I wouldn't do that, I believe you." She took out her purse and paid Little Jiang the full five day's wages. Little Jiang accepted them and flourished the notes in her hand: "Thank you, Aunt Xiao, your beds are really comfortable, when I lost my job a little while ago I had nowhere to live and I hadn't washed for a week nor had I had a decent meal. These last few days here have been a rest-cure!"

So Little Jiang had used her home to recuperate.

Little Jiang opened the door, waved dismissively at Xiao Ying and stalked off. Xiao Ying stood there transfixed, watching Little Jiang's back disappear into the lift.

Xiao Ying sat her mother up and dressed her in a purple woollen nightgown. She brought hot water and carefully washed her face and rinsed out her mouth. Ling Deqing's eyes watched her daughter's face throughout. She had seen Little Jiang the housekeeper pack up and go without even saying goodbye. Ling Deqing knew what had happened. Xiao Ying was full of anxiety, this morning she would again have to ask for time off to go to the domestic agency.

Chapter XX
Lost Love Reaches the Heights

Ling Deqing's eyes were fixed on her daughter's face, detecting the anxiety in it. After washing her mother's face, Xiao Ying went to the kitchen, filled a bowl with oatmeal porridge and brought it back. Ling Deqing extended her right hand and gestured that she wanted to write.

Write? Of course, Wei Le bought you a note tablet! Xiao Ying remembered that when Wei Le had seen that his grandmother's speech was blurred but the movement in her right hand was relatively good he had bought her a writing tablet at a school supplies shop. He though that through a combination of speech and writing she could make her meaning clear.

Xiao Ying put down the bowl of porridge and fetched the tablet from Wei Le's computer desk. A blue marker pen was attached magnetically to the bottom right of the white tablet in its pale green frame. At the bottom left there was a cartoon picture of a little ox—Wei Le knew that grandma had been born in the year of the Ox. Wei Le had shown his grandmother how to use it when he had brought it home. The magazine sized tablet was convenient to write on and was placed on Ling Deqing's chest. Ling Deqing looked at it happily and immediately wrote:

"Thank you" in large characters on it. Wei Le was proud of his idea and said to his grandmother: "When I come home on Friday, you can use this tablet and we can talk about all the interesting things that have happened at university." Ling Deqing was delighted and wrote "Study hard" on the tablet.

During the last few days however, Xiao Ying, distracted by anxiety over Little Jiang the housekeeper had forgotten the tablet. Ling Deqing had remembered, it was a present from her grandson.

Ling Deqing took the pen that Xiao Ying handed her and wrote: "Zichen?"

Xiao Ying said: "Dad's in his own room."

"?" Ling Deqing wrote a question mark on the tablet.

Ever since Ling Deqing had come home Xiao Zichen had stayed obediently in his own room only daring to emerge for meals. Xiao Ying was frightened that the sight of him would anger her mother. Her father had caused her illness, if he had not gone back home that day and not slept with Liu Qin's photograph clasped in his arms, he would not have provoked mother into burning those letters and she would not have had a stroke.

Above the door in Xiao Zichen's room was a three point provisional agreement that Wei Le had made with him and which he looked at several times a day. When he emerged for meals he always glanced at Ling Deqing's door from a distance and asked his daughter: "How's mother?" Xiao Ying replied: "Mother's well but you mustn't disturb her."

Xiao Ying thought that for mother herself to be this ill and yet to ask after father, made her truly the sort of person who had considered others all her life. She explained to her mother: "We thought dad might make you angry, so we made him stay in his room quietly reading and watching television."

Ling Deqing wrote another large question mark: "?"

Xiao Ying failed to understand the question mark and said: "We were going to put him in an old people's home, but he wasn't willing. I think we'll persuade him over time."

Ling Deqing frowned and laboriously wrote: "Did you consult me? Ask him—to come!"

Fearing that her mother would scold her father, Xiao Ying quickly said: "Dad wanted to come and see you and to come and see you in hospital but we thought you would be angry and didn't let him."

Ling Deqing looked at Xiao Ying and closed her eyes. Shortly after, Xiao Zichen followed his daughter in holding a copy of *English Language World*. He had been reading in his room and had jumped up from his chair when he heard Ling Deqing call him.

"Mother, a bit better?" Xiao Zichen stood timidly at the door not daring to enter.

"Very well." Ling Deqing smiled and nodded.

"They wouldn't let me come and see you." Xiao Zichen pointed at his daughter in grievance: "They made me stay in my room all day." Xiao Zichen burst into tears like a child.

"Aiya! Dad's come over all hard done by." Xiao Ying hurriedly pulled a tissue from the bedside table, wiped her father's tears and said: "I really didn't think you'd make a case of it! Don't cry, it'll upset mother!"

Xiao Zichen tried to stop crying but the tears trickled on. Xiao Ying wiped again and again, what must he have been thinking these last few days? We've all been so busy since mother came home that he's been neglected.

Ling Deqing's eyes were moist and she wrote on the board: "Zichen can feed me and Yingying can go to work."

Get father to feed mother? This really was a good idea! Xiao Ying thought happily, father's sound in wind and limb and mother's clear-minded, they match very well. If dad can help mother that would be the perfect solution.

Naturally, as soon as Zichen heard that Ling Deqing wanted him to feed her, his face was stained with tears again but he smiled: "Good, good, I'll feed you." He at once put down his magazine on the sofa, took up the bowl of porridge and seated on the edge of the bed took a spoonful of porridge, gently blew on it and carefully transferred it to Ling Deqing's obediently open mouth.

"Does it taste nice?" Xiao Zichen asked. "Yes," Ling Deqing nodded.

A ray of sunlight from the east window fell on Ling Deqing bathing her purple nightgown in a warm light, her face wreathed in a happy smile.

Xiao Ying looked on happily, Zichen's careful and considerate movements as he fed Ling Deqing made a heart-warming sight. Mother had worked for this family all her life and she had always seen her looking after dad, never dad looking after her. As Xiao Zichen transferred the second spoonful Xiao Ying's eyes filled with tears, it was both moving and sad. Mother cared about father, how was it that none of them had ever realised it? If mother could forgive father they could live together happily.

With dad looking after mother, Xiao Ying could happily go off to work. Nevertheless, she would first have to go and find a housekeeper.

Before she left Xiao Ying printed out a list for her father, 1, 2, 3, 4, 5, like a list of domestic tasks that set out things that had to be done and paid attention to.

Xiao Ying left. The old fashioned wall clock struck nine and the early morning bustle of the Pushi Apartments subsided. People going to work had all left and the elderly who had been out exercising had returned. Those who had bought vegetables from the market had sorted and washed them and they were drying in baskets in the corridors. Housewives who had swept and dusted doors windows tables and chairs, were sitting down to draw breath and rest. The faint sound of television could be heard from each home, Beijing and Shanghai opera as well as the noise of television serials.

In 706 Pushi Apartments Xiao Zichen was both happier than anyone and busier than anyone. He bustled in and out of Ling Deqing's room with tea and water for her. He washed her hands and face and scrubbed clean towels. He helped her to sit up and to lie down. He felt that he was the most useful person in the world and the happiest person in the world as well. Unconsciously, as he busied himself, he crooned the American song:

> I had a dream the other night
> Everything was still
> I dreamed I saw Susannah
> She was comin' down the hill
>
> Buckwheat cake was in her mouth
> The tear was in her eye
> Says I'm comin' from the South
> Susannah don't you cry
>
> Don't you cry for me oh Susannah
> 'cause I come from Alabama with my banjo on
> my knee ...

Ling Deqing gave a happy smile as she heard the sound of singing and her eyes were fixed on the form of Xiao Zichen as he hurried in and out. When he had had finished and just sat down he caught sight of Xiao Ying's list on the desk, with its detailed tasks:

1. Yingying has gone to work, will pass by the domestic agency find a housekeeper and bring her straight back.

2. Wenzhang has a class and a departmental meeting in the afternoon. He will come home as soon as it is finished.

3. Mother's lunch is a bowl of chicken broth and half a small bowl of candied lotus root and jellied fungus, two minutes in the microwave. Feed mother at 11:30.

4. Xiao Zichen's lunch is in a dish, fried egg rice with soy beans, chicken wings and a spare rib. Eat after three minutes in the microwave.

5. The nurse from the district hospital is coming this morning at 10 to sterilise the catheter. When dad hears the bell he must go and open the door.

6. If there's anything at all that is not clear, ring Yingying straight away.

Written at the bottom, in eye-catching large black Arabic numerals, was Xiao Ying's mobile number.

Xiao Zichen looked at the old-fashioned clock on the wall, 9:35, for the moment, he had nothing to do. He sat on the sofa by Ling Deqing's bed looking at a copy of *English Language World*. Ling Deqing withdrew her hand from beneath the quilt and gently prodded him. Xiao Zichen started and asked: "What does mother want to do?" Ling Deqing gestured that she wanted to write. Xiao Zichen quickly fetched the tablet and wiped it clean. Ling Deqing wrote: "What are you looking at?"

Xiao Zichen said: "I'm looking at *English Language World*."

Ling Deqing wrote: "Read to me."

Excellent, Xiao Zichen was delighted, apart from Wei Le, nobody normally much cared what he read. He sat upright, cleared his throat, was about to read and then asked: "This is in English and Chinese, which do you want?"

Ling Deqing wrote: "Both."

Good! This issue contained Xiao Zichen's favorite Yeats' poem, *When You are Old and Grey*. He read the English first, very slowly, with carefully controlled cadences and full of feeling. Ling Deqing eyes never moved, this was a poem that she knew well. After he had finished, Xiao Zichen asked: "Did I read well?" Ling Deqing nodded: "Really well!"

Xiao Zichen proudly stood up and read the Chinese translation that was alongside:

> When you are old and grey and full of sleep,
> And nodding by the fire, take down this book,
> And slowly read, and dream of the soft look
> Your eyes had once, and of their shadows deep ...

The look in Ling Deqing's eyes softened extraordinarily, and a smile hovered at the corners of her mouth. Intoxicated with his recitation, Xiao Zichen continued, luxuriant in tone and feeling:

> How many loved your moments of glad grace,
> And loved your beauty with love false or true,
> But one man loved the pilgrim soul in you,
> And loved the sorrows of your changing face;
>
> And bending down beside the glowing bars,
> Murmur, a little sadly, how Love fled
> And paced upon the mountains overhead
> And hid his face amid a crowd of stars.

When he had finished, Xiao Zichen did not forget to give the author's date of composition: 1893, or add the translator's modest *yi you wei jin*—meaning not fully expressed. He carefully considered the text: "This translation is by Fei Bai[1], I don't know him. I prefer Yuan Kejia[2], he translates quite well."

Ling Deqing did not respond. Xiao Zichen looked up and saw that tears were flowing down Ling Deqing's cheeks, falling drop upon drop on to the pillow.

"What is there to cry about?" he asked hurriedly. He had only been concerned with reading, word by word and phrase by phrase and consequently had not discovered the hurt to Ling Deqing. Why so hurt? He didn't understand and could only help her by wiping her tears with a paper napkin as he asked: "Qing, where does it hurt? Qing, Qing, don't cry!"

The use of "Qing" only deepened Ling Deqing's misery and the tears flowed like a burst dam. Xiao Zichen was at a loss, he knew that he had made yet another mistake but did not know where it lay, he stammered: "I'm sorry, Qing, I've made you cry!"

Ling Deqing shook her head vigorously, reached out and

---

1   Born in 1929.—*Trans.*
2   Born in 1921.—*Trans.*

grasped the hand that Xiao Zichen was using to dry her tears, looking at him through blurred eyes: "I remember this poem!" Xiao Zichen nodded: "I remember too." It was the poem that they had read together countless times when they had been in love.

Ling Deqing's soft hand grasped Xiao Zichen's thin one. Xiao Zichen hesitated a moment and then leaned over and gently implanted a kiss. Ling Deqing trembled and a blush spread over her face.

At that moment, Ling Deqing thought that she was content to die. She no longer needed the memories of the past or wanted to listen to every sound of that expansive life beyond the window. She just wanted the joy of that moment.

The doorbell played the tune of *Just Wait a Minute*. This was one of the tasks delegated by Xiao Ying and Xiao Zichen rushed to open the door. The nurse from the district hospital had arrived to sterilize Ling Deqing's catheter. This time Ling Deqing acquiesced and did not struggle.

In no time at all the nurse had sterilised the catheter. As she left she heaped praise on the cleanliness of the household and the fact that there was no odor from the patient's body, Good, excellent! The nurse gave the thumbs up to Xiao Zichen, this elderly couple, so effective at this sort of time and such true feeling!

Xiao Zichen's eyes crinkled in a smile as he listened. A smile played round the corners of Ling Deqing's mouth as she pursed her lips.

Chapter XXI
Translucency and a Poached Egg

The district hospital nurse had come and gone, tranquility had returned to number 706.

Ling Deqing prodded Xiao Zichen, she wanted to write.

She picked up the pen and wrote on the tablet: "Poached egg."

Xiao Zichen asked: "Do you want to eat one?"

Ling Deqing nodded and wrote: "Soft with a little salt."

Xiao Zichen said: "Good, good, I'll poach one for you, I can poach an egg."

Xiao Zichen went out and a little later returned frowning. He stood at the foot of the bed.

Ling Deqing gave him a questioning look: "What?"

"There's a notice over the door: 'Xiao Zichen must not turn on the gas'." Xiao Zichen pointed to himself: "Xiao Zichen, that's me."

Ling Deqing smiled, pointed to herself and wrote: "I'm here, I give permission."

Xiao Zichen turned and went into the kitchen. There was some clattering and in the twinkling of an eye he returned bearing a delicate blue and white bowl. Half leaning against the bed, Xiao Zichen helped her sit up and held the bowl in front of her with both hands. Ling Deqing saw a round white poached egg with a translucent yellow yolk floating in the bowl, the gleaming white and the sparkling yolk floating gently to and fro in the limpid soup. Ling Deqing took a deep breath and inhaled, the flavor of wine seeped into her heart. Seated on the side of the bed, Xiao Zichen blew away the heat and mouthful by mouthful, patiently fed the poached egg to Ling Deqing.

Xiao Zichen thought of something and suddenly said: "You've also fed me."

Ling Deqing knew what he meant. During the early days of the Cultural Revolution, Xiao Zichen had been locked up in the "cow pen" because of his "worship of overseas and fawning on foreigners". Ling Deqing had taken food to him at school. The Red Guard "little generals" had glared at her and refused to say where he was detained. Ling Deqing had not given up and had stayed standing at the school gate. She suddenly saw a female Red Guard wearing an arm band, the daughter of a neighbor in Pushi Apartments whose mother often consulted her on medical matters and with whom she was on good terms. Ling Deqing stopped her and the girl secretly took her to the school's physics lab where Xiao Zichen was locked in the male toilets, his bound hands red and swollen. In great distress, Ling Deqing had half knelt and fed Xiao Zichen spoonful by spoonful. Both of them had wept ... Ling Deqing nodded, she remembered, how could she forget?

After eating Ling Deqing beamed with satisfaction. Xiao Zichen wiped her mouth with a tissue. Ling Deqing said thank you and wrote: "It would be nice to have some foxnuts." Xiao Zichen said: "I like foxnuts too, I'll ask Yingying to go to Suzhou and buy some." Ling Deqing shook her head and wrote: "We mustn't trouble Yingying." Xiao Zichen nodded: "Yes, yes. Yingying has too much to do."

Ling Deqing pointed at Xiao Zichen: "You eat too." Xiao Zichen swallowed: "Yes, I'd like a poached egg."

Xiao Zichen helped Ling Deqing lie down, went into the kitchen, put a little water in the milk pan and put it on the gas stove. The water boiled, he opened the fridge door, took out an egg tapped it on the side of the pan and the yellow yolked egg plopped into the boiling water.

The telephone rang. Xiao Zichen dashed into the living room and picked it up: "Hello, hello!" It was his daughter. Xiao Zichen was delighted and anxious to boast of what he had accomplished.

Xiao Ying had been to a domestic agency. Three middle-aged women and two girls had been sitting there, one of whom had been Little Jiang. When she saw Xiao Ying she smiled at her without a trace of shame and just bent her head and fiddled with her mobile. Xiao Ying was rather embarrassed, she thought that not knowing where Little Jiang was off to recuperate next, she really should not have paid the introduction fee for her last time. She asked the assembled housekeepers about conditions but they shook their heads, they all wanted to be paid by the hour, hourly wages were high. She did not want to discuss "an even better rate" with Little Jiang sitting there and had had to leave.

Xiao Ying stood in the road at a loss. Should she go to work or find another agency? Although you could say that today her father had been able to help her mother and that consequently she was easy in her mind, there were things, like turning her over at night, washing and toilet that were better done by a housekeeper. If she didn't find one today there would be no solution to these difficulties. She had to go to another agency. Whatever happened, she had to bring back a housekeeper today. Xiao Ying rang home as she walked.

"Yingying," said Xiao Zichen loudly, "I helped mother with a lot of things ..."

Before he could finish, Xiao Ying interjected: "Dad, did the nurse from the district hospital come?" "I think so," said Xiao Zichen. Xiao Ying said: "Dad, at half past eleven, heat mother's lunch, two minutes in the microwave, don't leave it in too long."

"I know!" Xiao Zichen said proudly. "Anyhow, mother ate a poached egg."

"What?" Xiao Ying was delighted. "Mother's better?"

"Much better," Xiao Zichen replied. "She's very cheerful."

"Hello, hello!" Xiao Zichen wanted to say more but his daughter hurriedly hung up, she had to go and find a housekeeper. Xiao Zichen replaced the phone and stood in the living room thinking: "What do I have to do next? That's it, go and tell Ling Deqing that Yingying phoned."

Xiao Zichen went into Ling Deqing's bedroom: "Qing, Qing!" He heard gentle breathing, Ling Deqing was asleep.

Mother was too tired, she should sleep. "And I've been hard at it," said Xiao Zichen. He sat down on the sofa beside the bed. When it came to it, he was 80 and had been on the go since early morning, that was a long time. His feet ached, he patted his leg and looked carefully at Ling Deqing's sleeping form. Her white hair trembled gently with her breathing and a smile of contentment played about the corners of her mouth, with a faint blush on her cheeks. Mother was really god looking! Xiao Zichen's heart was filled with admiration, he must cook another poached egg tomorrow. "Mother liked to add a little salt, she said salt brought out the flavor, I prefer sugar, runny yoked poached egg ..."

Xiao Zichen replaced Ling Deqing's hand beneath the quilt. Wave upon wave of drowsiness assailed him and very quickly he fell fast asleep on the sofa. He dreamed that he and Ling Deqing were walking, lost in a dense mist, along a path beside a lawn in the French Park, Ling Deqing's tiny hand clasped in his own, amidst the ripple of laughter ...

Chapter XXII
Sacrifice

Xiao Ying arrived at the domestic agency in a hurry. It was in an old fashioned alley opposite the Suzhou River. There was a temporary single-story building erected by the neighborhood committee at the entrance to the alley, with white walls and a black tarred felt roof. It had once been the neighborhood milk station. The milk lorries used to arrive in the middle of the night and the clanking churns of milk had been piled in the interior. At first light, residents going to market arrived to obtain milk on their ration cards. More people arrived as it got lighter and it became noisier. In recent years, the number of people ordering milk had declined and the milk station had fallen into disuse, its mission accomplished. Overnight it had become a domestic employment agency. The tiny room had been divided in two, an office with a couple of benches and a desk with a telephone: the other room was crammed with three bunks, a temporary lodging for housekeepers who had just arrived in Shanghai to look for work.

Xiao Ying had been here several times in search of a housekeeper and had once been scared by the sight of three or four people sitting crowded on to a single bunk, she feared that the top was too heavy and would come crashing down. A tap had been installed at the entrance to the agency with a coal briquette stove next to it, where the housekeepers could boil water to make instant noodles.

When Xiao Ying went in to the agency, the pot on the stove outside the door was puffing steam and it looked as if it were about to overflow. Xiao Ying shouted: "It's boiling over!" A little housekeeper dashed out of the adjoining room and hurriedly removed the lid, it was a soft white poached egg.

Xiao Ying walked past and then turned back to look, a poached egg? Her heart immediately sank, what was it that dad had just said on the phone? "Anyhow, mother's eaten a poached egg." Yes, that's what he'd said! Wei Wenzhang had gone to school, mother couldn't get up, who had poached the egg? Could it be dad? How could he have lit the gas stove? Could he have forgotten to turn it off?

Xiao Ying was vaguely disturbed, quickly pulled out her mobile and rang home. The phone rang and rang but nobody answered. What was up? Why was dad not answering, could he have gone to sleep again? Or was he in the bathroom? Dial again! She dialed several times and nobody answered. Dad, pick up now, Xiao Ying was in a panic and decided not to look for a housekeeper. She ran back, flagged down a taxi and rushed home, continuously dialing the number until she reached the entrance to Pushi Apartments. There was still no reply.

The palms of Xiao Ying's hands were wet with cold sweat.

The smell of gas, thick and pungent, spread like a specter through 706 Pushi Apartments. Silently and stealthily it spread from the kitchen, crept into the living room and then into Ling Deqing's bedroom ...

The telephone rang and rang. Ling Deqing woke up and looked around, why didn't Xiao Zichen answer the phone? Xiao Zichen was sitting asleep on the sofa. The telephone was on the desk by the bed, she couldn't reach it. Xiao Zichen was deeply asleep. Ling Deqing reached out and gently pushed him and pushed him again. He continued to breathe like one fast asleep, he was tired out this morning.

The telephone continued to ring ceaselessly. Ling Deqing guessed that it was her daughter, anxious about them. She knew how her daughter's mind worked.

Ling Deqing sniffed, what was the smell? Why was it so unpleasant? She became alert, something was wrong. It was the smell of gas!

Where had the smell of gas come from? Could it be that Xiao Zichen had forgotten to turn it off? It was poaching the egg! Xiao Zichen had poached the egg and then gone to sleep himself. Ling Deqing was desperate, she pushed at Xiao Zichen with every ounce of strength in her body, but to no avail, she had not the strength. Xiao Zichen stirred, mumbled: "Qing, I'm tired," and started snoring again.

Ling Deqing was alarmed. This was her fault. She knew that Xiao Zichen often forgot to turn off the gas. Poaching an egg for her in the excitement of the moment had been a mistake. Her head began to ache, she knew that the situation was bad, this was a sign of gas poisoning. Xiao Zichen could not be awakened, could he have been poisoned? He was nearer the door through which the gas was seeping he would breath it first.

Ling Deqing looked around, she had to think of something!

The out-dated gas stove, old fashioned beyond words, was not fitted with an extinguisher. Time and again she had asked her daughter and son-in-law to install one but they had been too busy and had not kept it in mind. They had always believed that with Ling Deqing to guard it, the home would be safe. But she had suddenly had a stroke and they had been busy and had even less time to take care of it.

They were not to blame! This was her fault, who asked her to want a poached egg? Sheer greed!

Ling Deqing struggled up in bed, she did not know what she could do but she had to do something.

With difficulty, Ling Deqing edged herself towards the side of the bed. Using her right hand to take the weight of her whole body she moved inch by inch to the edge of the bed until she fell on the floor with a thump, hit her head on the bedside table and saw stars. Ironically, the pain made her more clear-headed. She tugged at the purple nightgown to straighten the nappy on her lower body, her left hand and foot would not answer but her right hand and foot were stronger than they had been in hospital. Like an insect she wriggled slowly across the floor. Using her right elbow she poled herself forward, inch by inch and foot by foot until, finally, she pulled open the bedroom door.

A thick gust of gas swirled towards the door. To prevent Xiao Zichen breathing in even more gas she pushed herself up, turned back, grasped the bottom of the door frame and then bit by bit forced the door closed.

It was as if all the strength that Ling Deqing had accumulated during the course of her life had been in preparation for this moment. Zichen mustn't die, Zichen mustn't die! Ling Deqing recited silently to herself. She realized that she was no longer of any use whatsoever to this world but Xiao Zichen was. He could sing, he could recite poetry, he could be a teacher at the English Salon in the park, Xiao Zichen must live.

Ling Deqing exerted all her strength and edged towards the living room door, the smell of gas in the living room was even stronger, her head was splitting, she saw stars and her body trembled slightly. Her stomach was churning and she was assailed by waves of nausea. Her hand was becoming weaker and every inch of movement required immense effort.

The closer Ling Deqing got to the kitchen the more widespread was the gas. She buried her head in the crook of her arm and drew breath, prone on the floor and motionless. She gathered up her remaining strength for a final push.

In this moment of rest a thought flashed through Ling Deqing's mind, was this an opportunity bestowed upon her by God to resolve her wish not to be a burden upon her daughter and to gently leave the human world? Could it be that she could make the final sacrifice for Xiao Zichen, the only man in the world that she had ever loved?

Ling Deqing raised herself and crawled forward again, closer, closer, she looked solemnly forward.

Happy are those who can control the end of life!

The telephone rang again, it must be Yingying. Ling Deqing longed for a final word with her daughter but she couldn't reach the telephone on the tea table in the living room not far from her. "Zichen, Zichen," she mumbled to herself, "you wretch, you mustn't go on sleeping."

Finally, after what seemed like the passage of a century, Ling Deqing reached the kitchen. The smell of gas was playing havoc in the kitchen. She saw the stove and saw the gas tap. Distantly she saw the overturned milk pan. She edged forward, another two feet and she could reach the gas tap. Zichen, you are saved!

But no matter how she struggled, Ling Deqing could not cover those last two feet, and could not reach the gas tap. Her hand answered less and less. She ordered herself: "Raise your hand, raise your hand!" She had a splitting headache, her body felt heavier and heavier, her neck stiffer and stiffer and her churning stomach vomited.

Ling Deqing's hand fell, its strength drained, her head fell with a thud on the concrete of the kitchen floor but she felt no pain.

The telephone rang again and Ling Deqing moved slightly, seeming to see her daughter's anxious expression. Yingying, I'm sorry, I've made a mistake, go quickly and save your father ...

The ear-splitting sound of the doorbell roused Ling Deqing: "Ah, Just Wait a Minute? Why wait a minute? Open the door quickly Yingying, you have a key!"

"Mum—mum!"

This was the last sound that Ling Deqing ever heard, but that happiest and most beautiful of sounds in the world was so sad and so heart wrenching. That shriek from her daughter seemed to have come from the very ends of the earth to tear body and soul asunder!

Xiao Zichen was saved! Ling Deqing's eyes closed and a sweetness welled up in her throat.

That *Just Wait a Minute* doorbell is really good, it woke me so that I can hear the word "Mother" as I leave ...

Chapter XXIII
You Know, She Loved Me

After treatment in a high pressure oxygen chamber, Xiao Zichen miraculously returned to life. Ling Deqing, however, had departed this world for ever.

It was Ling Deqing who had given Xiao Zichen his life back. When Ling Deqing had crawled from the bedroom and then forced the bedroom door shut, obstructing the flow of gas into the room she had prevented Xiao Zichen from inhaling a fatal dose. Ling Deqing, the former hospital matron, had thought of many ways of leaving the world so as not to encumber her family but she had not thought of putting an end to her life with one as awful as this. Her wish had been fulfilled but Xiao Zichen had been desolated by the loss.

The Xiao Zichen that emerged from hospital was a changed man. The gas poisoning had increased the obstruction of his cognitive ability. He didn't like conversation and his mood was apathetic. Apart from eating and sleeping he mostly sat expressionless. His hands held two objects: the copy of *English Language World* and the note tablet with Ling Deqing's writing on it. He held them to his chest and when he went to sleep at night put them on his pillow. He gazed for hours at the fragmentary sentences that Ling Deqing had left, weeping suddenly or smiling suddenly.

"What are you looking at?"

"Read to me."

"Both."

"I remember this poem."

"Poached egg, soft with a little salt."

"I'm here, I give permission."

"It would be nice to have some foxnuts."

"We mustn't trouble Yingying."

"You eat as well."

Xiao Ying guessed from the final fragments left by Ling Deqing that the last morning her mother and father had spent together had been made up of moments of comfortable warmth. Dad had recited a poem for mother and the poem had been in *English Language World*. Mother had eaten a poached egg that dad had cooked, soft with a little salt. Dad had not dared turn on the gas but mother had given him permission; mother had said that Yingying was not to be troubled, her heart ached with love for her daughter; mother had told dad to cook a poached egg for himself but he hadn't finished cooking it and had returned to mother's room and fallen asleep, leaving the poached egg in the pan. The water containing the egg white had boiled over putting out the flame and then the gas had wreaked its destruction.

From her father's disconnected and piecemeal remarks Xiao Ying gathered that the final morning that her parents had spent together had been one of sweet tenderness and that they had loved each other once again. The love had not been their previous love but *en ai*, a deep affectionate love. She had researched these two words in detail, within the character *en* there was *da*, the character for "large", so *en* was greater than love; *en* also contained *xin,* the character for "heart", so *en* was a support to the heart. *En* and *ai* each contained a heart, this was mutual harmony.

Wei Wenzhang would never forgive himself, he did not dwell on the failure to install an extinguisher on the gas stove but realized that his immersion in abstract sociological theory had led to this tragedy. Neither would Xiao Ying ever forgive herself. If she had kept on Little Jiang for a few days, her mother would not have died; if she had been determined and put her father in an old people's home her mother would still be alive.

But no "if"! Had there been an if, that sweet tender morning full of love would never have occurred.

Pain attacked in waves. The moment she thought of the phrase "We mustn't trouble Yingying" written on the tablet she could not stop crying. Mother, why did you always feel that you were a trouble to us? It is us who were a trouble to you all your life. You wouldn't let me change places with you, so that for once, I was the mother and you the daughter so that for once I could love and look after you as you had loved us, why could you not simply accept it?

In accordance with Ling Deqing's will, Xiao Ying gave her mother's body to the Shanghai Medical College. She realized that whether she donated it or not she would suffer. If she donated it she would do so unwillingly and if she did not it would be against her mother's wishes. Caught between these two difficulties she should be worthy of her mother and hand over the devoted heart of an old medical worker.

A colleague, Lao Qiao, came to see her and Xiao Ying tearfully poured out the grief that she could not rid her heart of. Lao Qiao, broken hearted, wept with her. At the end, Lao Qiao dried his tears, patted Xiao Ying and said: "Think of it as mother having gone to rest. The ancients said death is going home, 'regard death as a return and disaster as good fortune'. Do you know what 'regard death as a return' means? Return means going home, our final destination is 'our residence of origin' our only real home. So your mother 'regards death as a return and disaster as good fortune'! When we are born we embark on a long journey and when we should go home, then we must go home. People of our age must learn how to live with death, in the way that an apple falls from the tree when it is ripe, you cannot prevent it, it's a natural law."

Learn to live with death?

Xiao Ying had never thought about this problem before. However, what Lao Qiao had said calmed her down.

Xiao Zichen's ability to look after himself declined, the best place for him was an old people's home. Xiao Ying made her final decision but she had to secure her father's agreement. Her mother was no more and her father was broken-hearted, she could not pile the insult of ice upon the injury of snow.

Finally, on the evening of a certain Friday, the four of them sat down to eat, without Ling Deqing at supper the atmosphere was bleak. Xiao Ying picked a piece of steamed salmon for her father: "Dad, eat, eat a little more!"

"You eat," said Xiao Zichen quickly, picking up a piece of chopped chicken for his daughter.

Xiao Ying sounded out her father: "Dad, didn't the hospital tell you last time that your condition made you suitable for an old people's home?"

Xiao Zichen nodded: "Yes."

"Well, dad," said Xiao Ying cautiously, "would you be willing to go?"

"All right." Xiao Zichen nodded again.

Xiao Ying was amazed, her father had agreed so readily, for her part though, she was a little uneasy: "Dad, the Joy and Happiness Home is very near here, Wenzhang, Lele and I can visit you at the weekends or bring you home here for a couple of days, what do you think?"

"Fine." Xiao Zichen put down his bowl and chopsticks, rose to his feet and went to his room.

When Xiao Zichen came out of his room, he was carrying the note tablet and the copy of *English Language World* containing the poem by Yeats. The three of them looked at him in surprise, unclear as to what he was going to do.

"Muma," said Xiao Zichen to Xiao Ying, "going to the old people's home."

Xiao Ying hugged her father and wept. Xiao Zichen didn't

quite recognize people and had called Xiao Ying "Muma" in Suzhou dialect. The only person in his life that he had called "Muma" had been his own long dead mother from Wujiang county in Suzhou. Xiao Zichen now felt that his long gone "Muma" was at his side. Nor did he quite recognize who Wei Wenzhang was and often called him uncle. He didn't even know Wei Le and called him "Didi".—younger brother.

That weekend, because his grandfather was going to an old people's home, Wei Le spent all the time in his grandfather's room talking to him in English. Memory was odd, grandfather was much more fluent when he spoke English and his memory was obviously better. Wei Le wanted to understand why was it that all the memories retained in Xiao Zichen's mind were of his youth? Why had the events of later years been forgotten?

What was the nature of forgetfulness? Biologically speaking, memory loss was cell death, a long process.

Wei Le wanted to take his grandfather to the English Salon in the park once more, to sing and recite poetry but to his surprise, Xiao Zichen shook his head and refused to go.

"Why?" Wei Le was curious, it was grandpa's favorite place.

Xiao Zichen clasped the tablet on which grandmother had written and said: "I want to be with mother."

Then, Xiao Zichen dragged Wei Le into the living room. Ling Deqing's funeral portrait stood on the mantlepiece. Ling Deqing looked at them both, smiling. Grandmother's smile was gentle and elegant, like a blue tulip with the scent of serenity. Grandmother was good looking, Wei Le had grown up with grandmother and had only known her as kind, nice, and proud; he hadn't known that she was so beautiful. Grandmother was wearing a purple flower-patterned blouse, her eyes sparkled and her gaze illuminated the room.

Xiao Zichen pointed to the portrait and said mysteriously to Wei Le: "I know who she is."

Wei Le said: "But that's grandma!"

Puzzled, Xiao Zichen asked: "Grandma?"

"Yes," Wei Le said. "She's my grandmother."

Xiao Zichen was bewildered, he couldn't sort out these relationships, but never mind, he then said in English with an air of obvious mystery: "Do you know, she loved me."

Wei Le, moist-eyed, hugged his grandfather and said: "Yes, grandpa, in this world, grandma loved you most of all, and loved us all …"

The next day, a Monday morning, Xiao Ying and Wei Wenzhang took Xiao Zichen to the Joy and Happiness old people's home. The former factory building on the Suzhou River had been converted to an old people's home, the facilities were new, new beds, new quilts, new wardrobes and new televisions. Outside there were little bridges over flowing water and shady green trees. Xiao Zichen stood beaming at the window, waving to his daughter and son-in-law, goodbye, goodbye!

Every weekend, Wei Le came to the old people's home to visit his grandfather. They preferred to converse in English. One day, Wei Le took his grandfather downstairs to visit the garden. Light clouds floated high in the sky, the sun was shining and the leaves of the Tong trees were floating to the ground. The chrysanthemums on the terrace were blooming, red, yellow, white, green and purple, all competing in splendor. Beside each plant there stood an eye-catching sign with its name: "Silver threaded pearl", "Clear spring in an empty valley", "Pearl curtain waterfall", "Valley oriole", "Green waves in spring water", "Rush flowers on the maple leaf" …

As Wei Le and his grandfather read these beautiful names they felt that they were very poetic. Xiao Zichen's train of thought gradually floated into the distance, he looked up at the sky and suddenly said: "I can do everything through him who gives me strength."

Xiao Zichen had taught Wei Le this phrase. Wei Le had looked it up and found that it was from the bible, it meant that all was possible through reliance on the strength of God. Wei Le asked: "Grandpa, do you believe in God?"

Zichen shook his head: "I believe in mother, mother saved me."

Wei Le's nose tingled, grandpa missed grandma and he missed grandma a lot too. Grandma, you left too hurriedly, without a final word to me! The tears welled up in Wei Le's eyes and flowed unstoppably.

"Didi, don't cry!" Xiao Zichen reached out and dried his tears. "Didi, there, there!" But Xiao Zichen himself began to cry.

Wei Le and Xiao Zichen stood in the garden wiping away the other's tears of longing and desolation.

"Lethe!" Xiao Zichen exclaimed grief-stricken. "Lethe!"

"What 'Lisi'?" Wei Le asked. Grandpa frequently burrowed into the vocabulary of English and his train of thought skipped about, here one moment and there the next.

"Lethe!" Xiao Zichen said again. Wei Le took a pen and made his grandfather write it down. "What does it mean?" he asked.

Xiao Zichen wrote and said: "This is oblivion."

Why had grandpa suddenly thought of this word? Wei Le asked: "Grandpa, are you afraid of forgetting?"

Xiao Zichen nodded.

"Grandpa, what are you most frightened of forgetting?"

"Qing," Xiao Zichen replied earnestly, adding, "mother."

"Grandpa," replied Wei Le greatly moved, "how could we forget grandma? Grandma's love cannot be forgotten. You have not forgotten and I have not forgotten, nor have mother and father. Grandma was the best person in the world and she will be in our hearts for ever. Grandpa, if you do forget, I shall remind you, I swear."

Xiao Zichen smiled: "Good, good. You can remind me."

Back at home, Wei Le went on his computer, searched the net and found several hundred thousand hits for "Lethe": to forget, forgotten, a state of oblivion, the river of forgetfulness …

… In ancient Greek mythology there were five rivers in the underworld, the rivers of suffering, lamentation, lava, remorse and the river of forgetfulness. If, after death, you drink the water of the river of forgetfulness then you utterly forget your previous life.

... The god of sleep lives in a cave beside the river of forgetfulness and induces the inhabitants of the underworld to drink the waters of forgetfulness. No sunlight shines in the cave the whole year, only the faint glimmer of dawn and the shadows of dusk. The river Lethe flows through the bottom of the cave. Poppies and sleep inducing herbs grow at the entrance to the cave ...

... The mysterious Meng Po lives by the Bridge of No Return brewing pot after pot of Meng Po's potion. Meng Po gathers up the bits of forgotten memory and hangs them on the trees and flowers beside the river to form the fragmentary memories of ghosts. Every leaf and flower holds the story of a life. Every so often, Meng Po plucks a fragment and carefully tastes it or quietly listens in joy or despair ...

The West's river Lethe and Meng Po's potion in the East comprise a vocabulary of oblivion that contains countless mournful and yet beautiful tales that each follow the other. The East's mythology of forgetfulness has added a layer of colour filled with grief to the world.

Chapter XXIV
He Wept on the Banks of the Suzhou River

Very early on Saturday morning, Xiao Ying was still asleep and dreaming that her father was on a bridge in the distance and calling to her. The bridge resembled Zhapu Road Bridge but was also like one of the stone bridges in the Suzhou countryside. She didn't know where it was and calling "Dad" flew towards her father. At that moment, the telephone rang and woke her with a start.

The telephone call was from the Joy and Happiness old people's home: "Is that Xiao Ying? So sorry to disturb you but your father Xiao Zichen disappeared early this morning. He wasn't in bed in his room and we've searched the home from top to bottom without finding him. We've reported him missing to the police. Could you please come over at once, we feel very ..."

Xiao Ying flung down the phone without listening further and jumped up. She woke her husband as she dressed, dashed out of the door and shook Wei Le: "Wei Le, quick, get up, we're going to the old people's home, grandpa's disappeared!"

The three of them dashed out in a flurry of anxiety. The clock pointed to six o'clock and the early winter chill struck them.

Xiao Ying found the duty manager, a middle aged woman

with a tear stained face, unaware of where she had made a mistake. The old people's home had a duty security guard on each floor and the main entrance was closed from nine o'clock until six the next morning, Xiao Zichen could not have gone out by himself. But they had searched every nook and cranny and there was no sign of him, could he have grown wings and flown away?

In the midst of this anxiety the telephone rang. It was the duty policeman at the station ringing to say that very early that morning, when it was still almost dark, an old man holding a small magazine and a note tablet had been sitting on the banks of the Suzhou River on the stretch of Guangfu Road West in Changning District. People doing early morning exercises felt that he was a little strange and fearing that something was wrong had spoken to him. The old man had said nothing and had just wept expressionlessly, reluctant to leave however much people had tried to persuade him.

Guangfu Road West? Xiao Ying couldn't understand it. How had father ended up there? But from what he was holding, it was clear that it was him. The three of them rushed off in one of the old people's home vehicles.

At some distance Wei Le shouted: "Grandpa! Grandpa's sitting over there!" Xiao Ying and Wei Wenzhang looked, sure enough it was Xiao Zichen! He was sitting on a bench in the park facing the Suzhou River with his back to them. Not far in front, white pleasure-craft were moored alongside a jetty, a modernistic jetty for pleasure-craft was taking shape here. Through the railings, the clear river water could be seen flowing slowly by. On the opposite bank, skyscraper after skyscraper sprouted from the flat land.

The three of them got out of the vehicle and rushed across: "Dad, dad!" Xiao Ying called. "What are you doing here? How did you get here?"

Xiao Zichen was sitting on a bench on the river bank, tears streaming down his face, clutching the writing tablet and a copy of *English Language World*.

"Grandpa!" called Wei Le. "What are you doing sitting here?"

Xiao Zichen raised his head, looked at his daughter, looked at Wei Le, looked at Wei Wenzhang and said: "I'm looking for mother!"

"Dad," Xiao Ying grasped her father's hand, as cold as ice in the chill early morning wind of the Suzhou River in the late autumn. Wei Wenzhang quickly took off his coat and draped it over Xiao Zichen's shoulders. Xiao Ying said: "Dad, mother's no longer with us, she's gone."

"Gone?" Xiao Zichen pushed away his daughter's hand. "Why didn't she tell me? We were going for a walk."

"Walk?" Xiao Ying asked puzzled. "To come so far for a walk? Dad, it's too cold, let's go back."

Xiao Zichen rose unwillingly to his feet, mumbling: "How can it not be here? How can it not be seen?"

"Grandpa, what are you looking for?" said Wei Le in English. Wei Le knew that when he talked English with his grandfather his train of thought became more active, he asked him what he was really looking for.

"St John's University," said Xiao Zichen.

"St John's," said Wei Le. "Grandpa, that's been gone for ages!"

"It's here, the bridge is still here!" Xiao Zichen pointed to the Suzhou River as he spoke.

"Oh, of course!" Wei Le suddenly realised. St John's University had been on the Suzhou River and was now the University of Political Science and Law, it was not far away to the front.

Xiao Zichen said: "Mother arranged to go boating with me."

Xiao Ying had heard her father say that when they had been courting, they had often gone for walks on the banks of the Suzhou River by St John's University. It was not far from the back gate to the university and there had been tea houses, eating stalls and ferry boats. Mother had not liked coffee, so dad had invited her to drink Biluochun tea at a tea house. After drinking it a number of times, dad, who had loved coffee had also come to love Biluochun tea. They often also eat Yangchun noodles and wonton here …

Father was hallucinating again and had cunningly escaped.

Xiao Ying was puzzled: "Dad, how did you get here?"

Xiao Zichen shook his head vaguely: "Don't remember."

Was there anybody who knew how Xiao Ziche had escaped from the closely guarded old people's home? Was there anybody who knew how he had managed to get to the Changning stretch of the Suzhou River several miles away? It was a real mystery.

Never mind how, everybody breathed a sigh of relief. Xiao Ying thought that since the former site of St John's University was so close, why not take father to have a look? She had originally intended to have him home for the weekend. Xiao Ying made the suggestion and Wei Le clapped his hands in delight. Xiao Zichen started to smile. They hailed a taxi and the four of them made their way along the Suzhou River to the university.

Like silk, the waters of the Suzhou River wind their way from Guajingkou on Lake Tai, flowing frolicsome and crystal clear through the Jiangnan canal to Suzhou and Kunshan and then with countless twists and turns into the Shanghai city district. Here, the river had flowed sluggishly over a distance of more than sixty miles for several centuries. It's silt had settled, its sediment containing all the rich experiences of the passing years, the river held too much of the bustle of the city. The river slowed and it entered the city, turning muddy and its 18 bridges stood spanning the Suzhou River like 18 guardians. The former site of St John's University stood on the river bend after it entered the city.

Wei Wenzhang sat in the front of the taxi and Wei Le, Xiao Zichen and Xiao Ying in the back. Wei Wenzhang turned round and said: "Dad, if you want to go anywhere let us know and we'll take you at the weekend, you can't go running around by yourself." Xiao Zichen nodded, yes, yes, while he looked, unblinking, out of the window in excitement.

Not since Ling Deqing had died had the family been so happy together. Taking Xiao Zichen to visit the campus of his youth and allowing him to savor the good things of the past was exceptionally beneficial to his well-being.

Wei Le put out his hand to relieve his grandfather of the

magazine and tablet but Xiao Zichen clasped them to his chest. "I'll look after them," he said earnestly.

"All right, grandpa," said Wei Le.

"You know, she loves me," said Xiao Zichen half mysteriously, half in satisfaction.

"Yes, grandpa, grandma loved you most of all."

As she listened to this exchange between Wei Le and his grandfather, Xiao Ying was both happy and sad, and asked: "Then, dad, did you really love mother?"

"Yes, of course," Xiao Zichen replied. "I love her!"

The taxi-driver glanced back at Xiao Zichen, feeling that this old man was rather lovable and could speak English as well. "What was he saying?" he asked.

"My grandfather said that he loves my grandmother," Wei Le replied proudly. The driver laughed, such an age and still so romantic. The driver thought that the family's mutual love was rather comforting.

Xiao Ying eyes filled with tears, father no longer spoke of "liking" mother as he had done before but now spoke of "loving" her! After the fierce wind and rain along this long twisting road, father had at last taken mother to his heart, how gratified mother must be in the after-life! Wei Wenzhang looked back at his wife from the front seat and exchanged a deep look with her. Wei Wenzhang had also been moved by Xiao Zichen and thought that truly beautiful memories were closest to the soul and had to do with love.

But, how had Xiao Zichen actually come to be so far away on the Suzhou River?

Once out of the taxi and through the gate Xiao Zichen was a changed man. Each time he saw one of the old St John's University buildings he was able to tell them something amazing. He spoke with increasing fluency.

"Bu Fangji!¹" Xiao Zichen suddenly said the name as he looked at the unplastered walls and red brick of the beautiful

---

1 F. L. H. Pott, 1864–1947.—*Trans.*

buildings, "he was president for 50 years!"

"President?" asked Wei Le. "Was he Chinese or a foreigner?"

"A foreigner, a missionary." Xiao Zichen replied.

"Sports Hall!" Xiao Zichen pointed to the imposing red brick tower and the flying eaves of the Sports Hall as a smile creased his face. The commemorative plaque at the base of the building could still be made out. Xiao Zichen proudly told Wei Le: "The first swimming pool in China, I learned to swim here." And then: "The first football team in China, here too!"

"Building No. 40!" Xiao Zichen looked at the secluded peace of the courtyard, the trees reaching to the sky like some mythical Peach Garden and suddenly said: "Sun Yat-sen visited here. What! How come Schereschewsky[1] Hall is now Taofen[2] Building?" Xiao Zichen looked at the long covered walk-ways, the deep grey brick walls and the reddish plank floors and said: "Looking at Zou Taofen's statue, I thought of something, yes, that's it, Zou Taofen was a graduate here, so was Lin Yutang, Rong Yiren …"

Just as the Suzhou River flows, so the years pass silently and incessantly. As Xiao Zichen recalled these events, redolent of the sediment of past glory, his speech was filled with the intoxicating fragrance of history. Who is interested in the recollections of an individual unless he is famous? But today, every single word that Xiao Zichen uttered was, as far as Xiao Ying and her family were concerned, an absolute joy.

Oh! Dad even remembered this! Dad even remembered that! How can it be? In spite of everything, he preserves so many beautiful memories. How many other treasures are there, floating in the oceans of his memory? Xiao Ying wanted to retrieve them all and write them down.

Even if these beautiful, and sad, memories can never become fossils in the rocks of national history, they should be handed down through the generations of this family.

---

1   S. I. J. Schereschewsky (1831–1906), one of the university's founders. —*Trans*.

2   Zou Taofen (1895–1944), revolutionary writer and publisher. —*Trans*.

Chapter XXV
An Endless Ceremony of Farewell

Xiao Ying's idea of recovering her father's memories came too late.

After returning from the banks of the Suzhou River, Xiao Zichen caught pneumonia and from then on his condition deteriorated.

That fine morning on the banks of the Suzhou River and the joy of re-visiting St John's University disappeared never to return.

In the race between memory and mortality, who will be the winner? Even science has not reached a conclusion.

The following days resembled an endless ceremony, a ceremony of farewell.

Slowly, one by one, Xiao Zichen said goodbye to his family.

Wei Le found his grandfather's and grandmother's wedding photograph in his mother's photograph album and took it to show his grandfather.

Xiao Zichen lay in bed, stared at it for a long time, pointed at Ling Deqing and said: "I know this one," and then pointing to himself, "do you know who he is?" Then, not without jealousy: "What's he doing with her?"

Wei Le grimaced and said: "That's you!" He fetched a mirror

so that Xiao Zichen could see himself and said: "Grandpa, the one in the photograph is you when you were young, the one in the mirror is you now."

Xiao Zichen was still dissatisfied, pushed the mirror away and said: "How can I look so old?"

Another day, Wei Le went for a walk with Xiao Zichen at the old people's home. Xiao Zichen pointed to a single-storied building behind the main building and said: "We can go and have some fun." Wei Le was puzzled, what fun could there be?

He followed his grandfather, pushed open the door to find that it was the dining hall of the old people's home. After lunch, the kitchen had been swept spotlessly clean and the pots, pans and bowls polished until they shone. There was not a soul to be seen.

Xiao Zichen threaded his way familiarly through the kitchen, took several turns and passed through a small dark storeroom to where there was a pair of double doors with a switch above. The switch opened the doors, and there lay a bustling main road! Wei Le was curious and scared: "Grandpa, how did you know there was a door there?"

Xiao Zichen smiled proudly but said nothing.

Wei Le understood it all. Grandpa had escaped through this side door in the dining hall. He had gone looking for grandma's footprints on the banks of the Suzhou River and for the St John's University that entwined his soul. "But," Wei Le asked, "how did you get so far?" Xiao Zichen pointed at the taxis in the street. Having found the door through which grandpa had escaped, Wei Le was still puzzled, where had grandpa found the money for the taxi fare? How had grandpa been able to tell the driver where he had wanted to go? If he would not say, it would remain a mystery for ever.

Wei Le hurriedly pulled his grandfather back in through the door. As they made their way back through the kitchen, Xiao Zichen asked mysteriously: "Do you want to eat? There's a lot of food here." He pulled open a fridge door and there was a blast of cold air. Inside, there was bowl upon bowl of left-over food: "When my belly gets hungry, I come down here for a meal." Wei Le was stunned.

The next day, the tradesmen's side door in and out of the dining hall was firmly sealed off and the main door to the dining hall was locked after meals.

From then on, Xiao Zichen never even came downstairs, he spoke less and less and his voice became weaker and weaker. He lay in bed all day, staring blankly at the ceiling. When he saw Xiao Ying, his mouth moved as if to say "mother"; when he saw Wei Wenzhang he might recognize him but was unable to get the words out; when he saw Wei Le, he just stroked his face affectionately. The doctor said that there were new blood clots in the brain, but the increase or decrease of blood clots could not alter the progress of his condition, for Xiao Zichen, one day was never better than the other.

In the end Xiao Zichen recognized nobody, said nothing and slept all day. Occasionally he woke, his open eyes with neither spirit nor light, a mere empty space that seemed to see but saw nothing. Each day, the blood flowed sluggishly through this body as it gradually lost its memory.

Xiao Ying no longer grieved, what would happen would happen, it was enough that her father was not in pain. Mother had departed too precipitately and they had had no opportunity to say goodbye, but now, Xiao Ying's farewell to her father was interminable.

The farewell ceremony had started the day her father had sat weeping on the banks of the Suzhou River, bidding farewell to his *alma mater* and to the scenes of his first love, the banks of the Suzhou River. While he still had some memory left, all his close friends had been to say goodbye.

The ceremony entered its final stage.

Wei Le brought his grandmother's funeral portrait from the living room and sat on the edge of the bed, waiting for Xiao Zichen to wake.

Xiao Zichen opened his eyes and looked, totally expressionless, at Wei Le.

"Grandpa!" Wei Le called him and stood the photograph up in front of him, Xiao Zichen remained indifferent. He saw nothing of what was before his eyes.

Miracles still happen. Suddenly, Xiao Zichen screwed up his eyes and focused his gaze on Ling Deqing's face, he reached out a hand and stroked it and with trembling hand and lip he called: "Mother—mother!" His voice was weak but Wei Le heard it.

Two muddy tears trickled from the corners of Xiao Zichen's eyes and fell on the pillow ...

These were the last words that Xiao Zichen ever uttered. The very last green leaf from the tree of his memory. Without the green-leafed twigs of memory all was desolation. There was to be no green in Xiao Zichen's remaining days.

Xiao Zichen had at last completed his ceremony of farewell.

Joy and sorrow had left Xiao Zichen far behind. From this moment on, his face remained expressionless. The note tablet and the copy of *English Language World* lay beside his pillow, he glanced at them occasionally, as if they had nothing to do with him.

Life comes to an end and memory vanishes without trace. The day memory disappears life is just left with the shriveled husk of the body. Memory is the flower of life and its loss the wilting of that flower. The years of flowers wither with the years. Life comes full circle, who can prevent it?

Tomorrow, the sun will rise again, it will be another dawn.

Stories by Contemporary Writers from Shanghai